The
$\mathscr{S}$PINNING
Heart

www.transworldbooks.co.uk
www.transworldireland.ie

The
*S*PINNING
Heart

DONAL RYAN

Doubleday Ireland

DOUBLEDAY IRELAND
an imprint of The Random House Group Limited
20 Vauxhall Bridge Road, London SW1V 2SA
www.transworldbooks.co.uk

First published in 2012 by Doubleday Ireland,
a division of Transworld Ireland
as a co-publication with The Lilliput Press, Dublin

This edition published in 2013 by Doubleday Ireland

Copyright © Donal Ryan 2012

Donal Ryan has asserted his right under the Copyright, Designs
and Patents Act 1988 to be identified as the author of this work.

A CIP catalogue record for this book
is available from the British Library.

ISBN 9781781620069 (cased)
ISBN 9781781620076 (tpb)

Addresses for Random House Group Ltd companies outside the UK
can be found at: www.randomhouse.co.uk
The Random House Group Ltd Reg. No. 954009

The Random House Group Limited supports the Forest Stewardship
Council (FSC®), the leading international forest-certification organization.
Our books carrying the FSC label are printed on FSC®-certified paper.
FSC is the only forest-certification scheme endorsed by the leading environmental
organizations, including Greenpeace. Our paper procurement policy can
be found at www.randomhouse.co.uk/environment.

Typeset in Electra.
Printed and bound by
CPI Group (UK) Ltd, Croydon, CR0 4YY.

8 10 9 7

This book is dedicated to the memory of Dan Murphy

The
SPINNING
Heart

Bobby

MY FATHER still lives back the road past the weir in the cottage I was reared in. I go there every day to see is he dead and every day he lets me down. He hasn't yet missed a day of letting me down. He smiles at me; that terrible smile. He knows I'm coming to check is he dead. He knows I know he knows. He laughs his crooked laugh. I ask is he okay for everything and he only laughs. We look at each other for a while and when I can no longer stand the stench off of him, I go away. Good luck, I say, I'll see you tomorrow. You will, he says back. I know I will.

There's a red metal heart in the centre of the low front gate, skewered on a rotating hinge. It's flaking now; the red is nearly gone. It needs to be scraped and sanded and painted and oiled. It still spins in the wind, though. I can hear it creak, creak, creak as I walk away. A flaking, creaking, spinning heart.

When he dies, I'll get the cottage and the two acres that's left. He drank out Granddad's farm years ago. After I have him buried, I'll burn the cottage down and piss on the embers and I'll sell the two acres for as much as I can get. Every day he lives lowers the price I'll get. He knows that too; he stays alive to spite me. His heart is caked with muck and his lungs are shrivelled and black, but still he manages to draw in air and wheeze and cough and spit it back out. I was left go from my job two months ago and it was the best medicine he could have got. It gave him an extra six months, I'd say. If he ever finds out how Pokey Burke shafted me, he'll surely make a full recovery. Pokey could apply to be beatified then, having had a miracle ascribed to him.

What reason would I have ever had not to trust Pokey Burke? He was young when I started working for him – three years younger than me – but the whole parish had worked for his auld fella and no one ever had a bad word to say much beyond the usual sniping. Pokey Burke was called after the Pope: Seán Pól, his parents christened him. But his brother Eamonn was not yet two years old when his parents brought the new baby home and he decided the new baby was Pokey and everybody agreed away with him and little Seán Pól was stuck with Pokey for a lifetime. And beyond, if he leaves anyone behind that will remember him or talk about him when he's gone.

I SHOULD HAVE KNOWN something was up the day last year when Mickey Briars came in asking about his pension. Did ye boys know we're all meant to be in a proper pension? We didn't Mickey. Ya, with some crowd called SIFF. A proper pension like, not just the state one. Tis *extra*. Mickey's left hand was outstretched. It held the invisible weight of what he should have been given but wasn't. He tapped out his list of ungiven things, a bony finger slapping on sundried, limeburnt flesh. There were tears in his yellow eyes. He was after being shafted. Robbed. And not even by a man, but by a little prick. That's what he couldn't get over.

He went over and started to beat the prefab door until Pokey opened it a crack and threw an envelope at him and slammed the door again, just as Mickey put his head down and went to ram him like an old billy goat. Mickey's hard old skull splintered that door and it very nearly gave way. Pokey must have shat himself inside. I want my fuckin pension you little prick, Mickey roared and roared. I want my fuckin pension and the rest of my stamps. Come out you bollocks till I kill you. For a finish he went on a rampage around the place, turning over barrows and pulling form-work apart and when he picked up a shovel and started swinging, we all ran for cover. Except poor innocent Timmy Hanrahan: he only stood grinning back to his two ears like the gom that he is.

Auld Mickey Briars lamped Timmy Hanrahan twice across both sides of his innocent young head before we subdued him. We locked Mickey into the back of Seanie Shaper's Hiace until he became more philosophical for himself. Then we left him out and we all dragged crying, bleeding Timmy up the road to Ciss's and fed him pints for the evening. Mickey Briars softened his Jameson with tears and told Timmy he was sorry, he was always fond of him, he was a grand boy so he was, it was only that he thought he was laughing at him. I wouldn't laugh at you, Mickey, Timmy said. I know you wouldn't son. I know you wouldn't.

Pokey had shouted after us to put the first round of drink on his slate. There wasn't a man of us put his hand in his pocket all evening. Poor Timmy puked his guts up early on in the session and we slagged him – good-naturedly of course – and he laughed through his snots and his tears and the blood on his head caked up grand and came off in one thin scab before we sent him walking home for himself with a bag of chips and three battered sausages and a dose of concussion that could have easily killed him.

To this day there's a quare auld draw on one of his eyeballs, as if it's not able to keep time with its comrade. But it makes no odds to Tim; if there's a mirror in that house he hardly pays it any heed. And if he's thicker than he was before, who's to say? Who's to care? You don't need brains to shovel shit and carry blocks and take orders from rat-faced little men who'll use you all day and laugh at you all night and never pay in your stamps.

That's the worst of the whole thing. We all went in to draw our stamps and they only laughed at us. Stamps? What stamps? There wasn't a stamp paid in for any of us, nor a screed to the Revenue, either. I showed the little blonde girl at the hatch my last payslip. You could clearly see what was taken out: PRSI, PAYE, Income levy, pension. She held it in front of her with her nose wrinkled up like I was after wiping my armpit with it. Well? I said. Well what? What's the story? There's no story sir. I wasn't on the computer as an employee of Pokey Burke or anyone else. Did you never look for a P60 from your employer? A what, now? You're some fool, she said with her eyes. I know I am, my red cheeks said back. I think she started to feel sorry for me then. But when she looked at the line of goms behind me – Seanie Shaper, innocent Timmy, fat Rory Slattery and the rest of the boys, all clutching their dirty payslips – she started to feel more sorry for herself.

TRIONA LETS ON she doesn't blame me for being taken for a fool. Sure why would you have ever checked, love? It wasn't just you. He fooled everyone. My lovely, lovely Triona, she fairly let herself down when she married me. She could have gone with any of them smart boys that got the real money out of the boom: the architects, solicitors, auctioneers. They were all after her. She went for me bald-headed though, as if to spite them. She put her hand in mine one night inside in town after the disco and that was that; she never let go of me. She saw more in me than I knew was there. She made me, so she did. She even softened my father. How did you pull her, he wanted to know. She won't stay with you. She's too good for you. You're her bit of rough, he said. All women goes through this auld phase. Ya, I thought, like my mother, except her auld phase didn't end until she died, twisted and knotted up and spent, exhausted, pure solid burnt out from him.

And now I can't pay for the messages. Christ on a bike. I had a right swagger there for a couple of years, thinking I was a great fella. *Foreman*, I was, clearing a grand a week. Set for life. Houses would never stop going up. I'd see babies like our own being pushed around the village below and think: lovely, work for the future, they'll all need their own houses some day too. We knew Pokey was a prick, but none of us cared. What matter what kind of a man he was, once the bank kept giving him money to build more and more? Once they buried that boy of the Cunliffes years ago and his auld auntie grabbed that land and divided it out among the bigshots, we all thought we were feckin elected.

That poor boy knew more than any of us. I remember when they carried him up to the Height, how the Penroses wheeled little one-legged Eugene out on to the street as he passed on his way to lie between his mother and father, and Eugene spat on the hearse and the big dirty gob slid down along the side window. He couldn't stop blackguarding that boy even and he dead. I remember him well. He got kicked around the place and all I ever did was laugh. He was the quietest boy you'd meet, he never threw a shape nor said a cross word, and he ended up getting shot down like a mad dog. And everyone was glad. We all hated him.

We all believed the newspapers, over the evidence of our own eyes and ears and a lifetime of knowing what we knew to be true. We wanted to hate him. He hadn't a hope.

I WAS as smart as any of the posh lads in school. I was well able for the English and geography and history. All those equations in physics and maths made sense to me. I couldn't ever let on I knew anything, though, that would have been suicide in my gang. I did pass maths even though I know I could have done honours. I never opened my mouth in English. A lad from the village wrote an essay one time and Pawsy Rogers praised him from a height; he said it showed great flair and imagination. He got kicked the whole way back to the village.

I had that King Lear's number from the start, well before the teacher started to break things down slowly for the thick lads: he was a stupid prick. He had it all and wanted more, he wanted the whole world to kiss his arse. I had Goneril and Regan pegged for bitches too, and I knew that Cordelia was the one who really, truly loved him. She wouldn't lie to him, no matter how much he wanted her to. You're a man and no more, she said, you're not perfect, but I love you. Cordelia was true of heart. There aren't many Cordelias in this world. Triona is one. I was scared before I knew I was, of facing down Josie Burke, and she told me. I was scared, imagine, even though I was in the right.

Pokey Burke left his father and mother to mop up after him. The auld lad said he didn't know where Pokey was, but I knew he was lying. He owes me money, Josie, I said. Does he now? Did he not pay you a fine wage? He was looking down at me from the third step before his front door. I might as well have had a cap in my hand and called him sir. My stamps. My pension. My redundancy. I could hear my own voice shaking. The state looks after all that when fellas goes bust, he said. Go in as far as town to the dole office. He said no more, only kept looking down at me, down along his nose. Right so. Right so, I will. I didn't say I'd been there already, we all had, and it turned out Pokey had rowed us up the creek and left us there. I should have said I'd been on to the taxman and the welfare inspectors and the unions and they'd soon soften Pokey's cough, but I hadn't and I didn't and I turned away with a pain in my heart for the man I'd thought I was.

Triona said don't mind them love, don't think about them, the Burkes were always users and crooks dressed up like the salt of the earth. Everyone's seen their real faces now. The whole village knows what they've done. You're a worker and everyone knows it. People look up to you. They'll be fighting each other to take you on once things pick up. Everyone around here knows you're the only one can keep the reins on them madmen. Who else could be a foreman over the lads around here? Who else could knock a day's work out of fat Rory Slattery? And stop Seanie Shaper from trying to get off with himself? I laughed then, through my invisible tears. I couldn't stand myself. I couldn't stand her smiling through her fear and having to coax me out of my misery like a big, sulky child. I wish to God I could talk to her the way she wants me to, besides forever making her guess what I'm thinking. Why can't I find the words?

Right so, right so, right so. Imagine being such a coward and not even knowing it. Imagine being so suddenly useless.

I THOUGHT ABOUT killing my father all day yesterday. There are ways, you know, to kill a man, especially an old, frail man, which wouldn't look like murder. It wouldn't be murder anyway, just putting the skids under nature. It's only badness that sustains him. I could hold a cushion or a pillow over his mouth and nose. He'd flail about, but I'd bat his hands softly back down. I wouldn't mark him. His strength is gone from him. I wouldn't like to see his eyes while I killed him; he'd be laughing at me, I know well he would. He'd still be telling me I'm only a useless prick, a streak of piss, a shame to him, even and he dying. He wouldn't plead, only laugh at me with his yellow eyes.

I was always jealous of Seanie Shaper growing up. Any time I ever called to Seanie's, I'd hear them laughing when I got to the bend before their house. They'd all be roaring laughing at some aping their father would be at, and their mother would be cooking and telling them to shut up their fooling but she'd be laughing herself. The odd time, I'd stay and eat, and Seanie and his brothers and sister would take ages to finish because they'd be laughing so much. Their father was wiry and kind-looking. He had a lovely smile. He'd warm you with it. You knew there was nothing in him only good nature. He had a big pile of old *Ireland's Own* magazines he'd look for when they had the dinner ate. He needed them for the song words. They'd all roll their eyes and let on to be disgusted but still and all they'd clap and sing along while he pounded out the songs: 'The Rathlin Bog' and 'The Rising of the Moon' and 'Come Out Ye Black and Tans'. It twisted my soul, the pleasure of that house, the warmth of it and the laughter; it was nearly unbearable to be there and to have half my mind filled with the chill and the gloom and the thick silence of our cottage. I hated Seanie Shaper for having a father like that and not even knowing his luck.

MY FATHER never drank a drop until the day the probate was finished on Granddad's farm. Paulie Jackman sent off a cheque that same day to the Revenue for the inheritance tax. He handed my father Granddad's savings in cash. Then my father went to Ciss Brien's and ordered a Jameson and a pint and drank them down and vomited them up and Ciss herself, who was still going strong that time, gave him a sog into the mouth of her experienced fist for himself. It took him months to train himself to be a drinker. He never wavered from his goal. He paid no heed to pleas or censure. He was laughed at and talked about and watched in wonderment by the old guard of Ciss's front bar; here was a man they always knew yet hardly knew at all, a quiet son of a small farmer who was never known for intemperance or loudness, a cute fucker they all thought, and he drinking out a farm. They loved him, or loved the thought of him, what they thought he was: a man who could easily have had a good life who chose instead their life: spite and bitterness and age-fogged glasses of watery whiskey in dark, cobwebbed country bars, shit-smeared toilets, blood-streaked piss, and early death. He could have helped it but didn't. They couldn't help it and loved him for being worse than them. He was the king of the wasters. He bought drink for men he didn't like and listened to their yarns and their sodden stories. He gave an eye filled with darkness they could mistake for desire to women he thought were only common whores. The day he spent the last penny that was got for the land he stopped drinking. It took him nearly five years to drink out the farm and when it was done he never took a sup again. He wasn't a drinker at all, really. The old guard were heartbroken after him. They couldn't understand it; he never looked at them again.

He drank out the farm to spite his father. It was the one thing Granddad said he knew my father wouldn't do, so my father did it. At least I can trust him not to drink out the farm, Granddad would say. It was the *at least* that galled my father, I'd say. It meant nothing and everything: Granddad was saying he was good for nothing, every badness was possible with him, but he didn't drink and never had, so at least there was that one thing, one thing only that could nearly be seen as a good thing. My father called his dead bluff. I walked him home from his last session. I haven't a bob left now, he said, and if we went over this minute to my father's grave and dug him up, he'd be face down inside in the coffin. And he laughed and coughed and laughed and pissed down the leg of his pants and laughed and fell in the cottage door and woke up sober the next day and was never drunk again a day in his life.

I can forgive him for turning piles of money into piss and for leaving my mother to her holy hell, too mortified to sit up past the back row in Mass; walking quickly, head down through the village, sneaking about her business for fear of being forced to talk to anyone; sitting crying tears of frustration out beyond Coolcappa in a crock of a car with a burnt clutch and a steaming engine and a screaming child in the back of it while he sat silently swallowing her claim to a life. I'll never forgive him for the sulking, though, and the killing sting of his tongue. He ruined every day of our lives with it. Drunk, he was leering and silent and mostly asleep. Sober, he was a watcher, a horror of a man who missed nothing and commented on everything. Nothing was ever done right or cooked right or said right or bought right or handed to him properly or ironed straight or finished off fully with him. We couldn't breathe right in a room with him. We couldn't talk freely or easily. We were mad about each other, my mother and me, but he made us afraid to look at each other for fear he'd want to know were we conspiring against him again. We stopped looking at each other for good for a finish and stopped talking to each other a few years later and the day we buried her I wanted to jump into the ground and drag her back out and scream at her to come back, come back, we'll walk to the shop and I'll hold your hand and we won't mind Daddy and I'll pick a bunch of flowers and leave them on your locker for you and if he calls me a pansy we'll tell him to feck off and we'll give back all these years of ageing and dying and stupid, stupid silence and be Mammy and Bobby again, two great auld pals.

I ALWAYS KNEW Pokey Burke was a bit afraid of me. Triona says I *exuded menace* when she met me first. She has a lovely way of putting things. There was no one stopping *her* doing honours English. She says I stood against the bar inside in the disco in town and stared at her. Her friend said what the fuck is that *freak* looking at, but Triona knew the friend was only raging I wasn't staring at her. Oh, don't look back, for Christ's sake, the friend said, he's from an awful family, they live in a hovel, the father is a weirdo and the mother never *speaks* – but Triona looked back all the same and when I scowled at her she knew I was trying to smile, and when I hardly spoke to her on the way home she knew deep down that I was terrified of the lightness and loveliness of her, and when she said are we going to shift so or what, I thought I'd never again regain the power of movement.

Pokey Burke had been mad after her; she'd shifted him weeks before, and he'd been rough, biting her lip and clawing at her bra, and I'd never forgive him for having touched her. Even when he told me I was foreman, and was handing me an envelope every week with twenty fifties in it, he was afraid of me, and I was afraid I'd kill him. But still and all he needed me, and I sneered at him, and we all called him a prick, but now he's beyond, sunning himself in God only knows where, hiding from the bank and the taxman and probably trying to ride foreign wans. And here am I, like an orphaned child, bereft, filling up with fear like a boat filling with water.

HAVING A WIFE is great. You can say things to your wife that you never knew you thought. It just comes out of you when the person you're talking to is like a part of yourself. We went to a play inside in town one time; I can't remember the name of it. You couldn't do that without a wife. Imagine it being found out, that you went to see a play, on your own! With a woman, you have an excuse for every kind of soft thing. The play was about a man and wife; they just sat on the stage on either side of a table, facing the audience, talking about each other. Your man was like my father, only not as bad. The wife was lovely; she was dog-tired of your man's auld selfish ways, but she persevered with him all the same. He sat there, drinking a glass of whiskey that was really red lemonade and smoking fag after fag, grinning back to his two ears as she read him to the audience. He had an auld smart reply for every criticism. They aged onstage, as they were talking. I don't know how it was done. For a finish, they were both old and their lives were near spent, and at the very last, your man turned around and admitted he thought the world of her; he'd always loved her. He put his hand on her cheek and looked at her and cried. Christ, your man was some actor. On the way home in the car, tears spilled down my face. Triona just said oh love, oh love.

Josie

I LOVE my first son more than my second son. I often wonder should I go to confession and purge that from my soul. But is it even a sin, to love one child more than another? It's wrong, all right; I know that. I gave my second boy everything, to try to make up for it: my business, years of my time showing him what to do, enough working capital to allow for all sorts of balls-ups. Poor Eamonn only barely got the money to pay for his digs above in Dublin when he went to Trinity. There's neither of them thick enough to not know where they stood, though. I was always stone cracked about Eamonn. I couldn't understand how I never felt the same about poor Pokey. I even let Eamonn take his name from him. *Pokey*, he said, and pointed a fat little finger at the new baby, and we all laughed and told him he was great, and Seán Pól was lost forever. He never got a look in, the poor little darling boy.

I should have come down from the top step when Bobby Mahon came here the other day asking to know where was Pokey and what was going to be done about stamps and redundancy and what have you. I should have taken his hand and shook it and told him how sorry I was it was all gone wallop besides snapping at him; I should have apologized to that man on my son's behalf. I snapped like that out of crossness with myself. I was too ashamed to look the man in the eye; Bobby Mahon, who never missed a day, who I was always so glad was foreman after Pokey took over – I thanked God there was a man there to keep Pokey from getting too big for his boots. Pokey was more than half-afraid of Bobby Mahon. He wished he *was* Bobby Mahon, I think. I have a feeling that he asked himself what Bobby would think of every decision he was making before he made it. It's only a shame he told no one he was mortgaging everything on the building of one last massive estate of houses that no one was going to buy and a share in some monstrosity beyond in Dubai. I should have shook Bobby Mahon's hand and thanked him, and apologized, besides leaving him walk off with his face red with anger and disappointment.

I think of Pokey and I feel disgust, with him and with myself. Wasn't it I reared him? Or maybe that's what went wrong; I left most of the rearing to Eileen. And isn't it a sacred duty, to rear your children? I got that all turned around in my head, of course. I confused providing for them with rearing them. I got a fixation on work and having enough money that waxed and waned for my whole adult life, but was always there. I never even really went into a shop and bought anything. Eileen buys my pantses and shirts and shoes and socks and underwear. I give out stink to her if I open the hot press and there's none at hand. I used to read her from a height at Christmas over the expensive presents. Lord God I'd take that back if I could. I'd give every single penny I ever had and more to go back to certain days and hours and change things just a little bit. I'd catch Pokey in time. I'd catch myself.

MY CHICKENS are gone woeful fat. Eileen says I leave them in too much corn altogether. She doesn't know that I also pick big caterpillars off of the cabbages and feed them in to the old fatsos. They see me coming and get into a right flap. They're the fattest, happiest chickens in Ireland, I'd say. I have a daughter too, you know. I can't bear talking to her any more. I used to think she was the bee's knees, but now I'd rather feed caterpillars to chickens than talk to her. What sort of a man am I at all? If you heard the rubbish she talks, though, about poverty and Palestine and carbon dioxide and Tibetan monks and what have you. And if you saw the cut of her – no bra, men's army pants, big auld boots – you'd rather look at chickens, too. I don't feel guilty about her at all. Isn't that awful?

I served my time in the sixties as a block-layer beyond in Liverpool, in a firm belonging to a great big fat fella from south Tipp. He was a horrible, ignorant man. I had no digs sorted out for myself when I got over there. He gave me my start on my first day off of the boat. I asked him where would I stay and he laughed at me, a big, fat, wet laugh. I don't know in the fuck, he said, and I don't care, once you're here in the morning at seven. I sat on the steps of a locked-up church all that night, frozen with the cold, and scared of every shadow. I wondered was it a Protestant church. I wondered what was the difference. I learnt my trade quickly, and didn't mess around. I hardly ever drank; it sapped the strength from men and made them forget themselves. I overtook that big fat man from Cashel. I went out on my own and put in for every job going. I brought four or five boys with me who I knew wouldn't argue with me. I undercut the prick all over Liverpool. He died of a heart attack at the door of a pub in Warrington. People stepped out over his body. I laughed when I heard. Then I thought more about it and felt sick. But at least my laugh had been heard and noted. I was hard.

I came home and never stopped working. I bought the yard and a site and built a house and bought machinery and married Eileen and worked and worked and worked. I never stopped going. All through the seventies and eighties, I hardly drew breath. I built a beautiful estate of bungalows on a lovely site when no one else was building private estates. It was I started all that. I fell into the drink one time, for about six months. To this day, I don't know why. I ended up trying to force myself on a woman. She got away from me easily enough. I laughed at her and went back to my drink and saw men looking at me with satisfaction in their eyes. I knew then to stop drinking. I often thought to find that woman I handled roughly and say I was sorry. I often wondered did she know I had a wedding ring inside in my pocket and a pregnant wife at home crying over me. I wonder does she hate me still.

JOSEPH BURKE was my father's name too. Second sons were named for their fathers in those days as a rule. Second sons got a name and first sons got everything else. My father made us all afraid of dishonesty. The devil loves lies, he always said. The devil loves liars. It wasn't from me that Pokey learned deceit. He never paid in those boys' stamps. Imagine that. I used to have that done every year before January would be out. The Revenue Commissioners are roaring for VAT, the sub-contractors are arriving to the door with invoices every day. Honest men, who know only work, white with the shock of the sudden stop that everything is after coming to. When I think about it, what people must be thinking and saying, I can hear my heart beat in my chest. I can feel a hardness, a tight pressure. I think of a hose with too great a flow through it, stretched and strained. Sweat starts to sting my forehead. Eileen says nothing. What's there to say? Her silence comforts me. If she blamed me, she'd say it. Who's to blame when a child turns rotten?

That's the thing though. Did he turn bad or did he start out that way? Either way it's my fault. There's no getting away from it. I'm the boy's father. His nature and his nurture were both down to me, when all is said and done. He got no badness from his mother, that's for certain. Eamonn and Pokey were always mad about each other as small boys. How's it they ended up so different? I did my damnedest not to make fish of one and flesh of the other; I counted out seconds in my head of time in my lap, the number of times I lifted each one up, the number of times I smiled at each one. Pokey had an unbelievable eye, though, to see a slight so small there was nearly none at all: he noticed every time I looked at Eamonn, patted his head, squeezed his little fat leg. He had a ledger inside in his head on which every single move I made was entered, and it never, ever balanced in his favour. I started resenting him, and nearly hated him. I did hate him. God forgive me, I should confess *that*. Imagine poor old John Cotter, how he'd stutter out my penance and redden every time I met him after. I'd nearly have to travel in to the Cistercians in the city, where my face would not be known or seen again. Or those Franciscan lads in Moyross: they'd have me right with God in no time. They'd never have me right with myself, though.

I haven't said a word yet to Eamonn about Pokey lighting out for the continent. He doesn't know about the big huge loan from Anglo, the Revenue, the lads' stamps, their redundancy, anything. I'm afraid of upsetting him. I'm ashamed opposite my own son to tell of his brother's badness. Eamonn teaches in the city. They're all pure stone mad about him in there: the other teachers, the young lads, his wife's people. Jesus, what if I hadn't him? I'll have to tell him soon. The next time he calls with Yvonne and the children, he'll ask as he always does, is Pokey coming, and I won't be able to lie to the boy. I hope I don't start to cry like a fool. My tear bags are fierce close to my eyes these days. That Bobby Mahon and my Eamonn are very alike in ways. They're both men you'd be proud of, who you'd be embarrassed opposite, having to tell of the failings of other men and feeling as though those failings are your own.

And there's no one can say the whole fiasco with the business wasn't my fault, that's for certain. It was I handed over all to Pokey. I only kept our house and my pension. But there were seven years there where you could build houses out of cardboard and masking tape and they'd be sold off of the plans. People queued all night to buy boxes of houses all crammed together like kennels. Pokey cleaned up. He paid me a dividend and I fattened on it. We should have known it would all end in tears. Around here, it all started with tears: that boy of the Cunliffes getting shot in his own yard by the guards, and his land going to his auntie, who shared it out among us like the Roman soldiers with Our Lord's purple robe. That was no way for good times to start.

Lily

WHEN I WAS inside in the hospital having my fifth child, a nosy bitch of a midwife asked me to know who was the father. I told her by accident. They had me drugged up to my eyeballs. The auld hag must have fattened on my answer. Bernie came down to my house a few weeks later. It must have taken that long for the whispers to reach his hairy ears. He charged in here like a bull. I remember smiling at him like a fool; I actually thought he'd come for a look at his child. He said nothing, only punched me straight into my face. Then he drew back his big fist and punched me again, right into my mouth. You stupid bitch, he said, you stupid, stupid bitch, I should kill you. My lip split open and pumped blood. My front tooth came out. Then he threw a twenty-pound note at me and charged back out. My eye swelled and closed and turned black. He never called to me again.

I met Jim Gildea the sergeant a few days later, in the Unthanks' bakery. He looked down at me as I waited for my sliced pan and he flinched; my face was still in ribbons. He didn't want to ask me and I didn't want him to. What happened you, Lily? I fell, Jim. I could see the relief on his face, and the knowing in his eyes of my lie. He was grateful for my lie; he'd think of it again.

THERE ARE rakes of men around here that have called to me. I've had years of eyes at my door. Eyes that can't meet mine, full of hunger when they arrive and full of guilt as they leave. Eyes full of laughter, thinking I'm only a joke; eyes full of tears. I've seen eyes full of hate, and I never knew why those men hated me. I'd never blame a man for calling to me. Men have to do what they have to do. Nature overpowers them. Some of the old farmers were lovely, once you got over the smell. They had a smell you could nearly talk yourself into liking. I even bathed one or two of them – they loved it – like big auld babas, splashing around and grinning up at me with their soft gums and their hard dicks. Cow shit is nowhere near as bad as dog shit, or human shit. A fella called to my door one time, hardly able to stand up for drink, with a toughie English accent and shit all over the tail of his shirt. He must have wiped his arse with it, in some dirty toilet. I ran him. I'd never be *that* stuck.

I was only about eleven when men started looking at me. There was something about me that they couldn't stop looking at. I grew up early. But lots of young girls grew up early in them days. There was something more about me that drew men's eyes. It was years and years before I knew what the word for that thing was. I was *wanton*. I had a wanton look about me. Do I still? I don't know in the hell. Hardly, I'd say. A young fella that I met on a lane in the forestry one summer's day told it to me years ago. I was looking for burdock; he was striding along with his white legs sticking out from his baggy short pants and a little knapsack on his narrow back. I had my eldest fella, John-John, with me; he was only small, whining and snotting along beside me, trying to copy the song I was singing and making me laugh. His father was a real gas card, too. I heard one time that he came a cropper beyond in Liverpool, off of a motorbike. There were too many years gone by for me to care.

I brought the skinny townie back to the cottage with the promise of a bag of mixed herbs from my little garden. He leapt on me the minute I had John-John put away into the back room to play with his toys. The babies were sound asleep. Christ, you're *wanton*, he gasped, as he finished, not even a minute later. I'm what, now? Then he told me what it meant, slowly and kindly, like I was a simple child. He called again from time to time over the years. I think I made him feel bigger and smarter than he was. He always took away a bag of herbs or a jar of preserves with him. *That's* what he was leaving the money for, in his own mind.

I ONLY EVER refused men who really and truly disgusted me. Men who you knew would prefer to force you even if you were willing. I only refused a good man once, because I knew his goodness well and was afraid of blackening his mind against himself. He had himself beaten out of shape. He didn't know himself. He was trying to be cold and unfeeling and bad, but he wasn't able to be that way; he was full of kindness that he thought was weakness. That's the way he was reared. He was pouring drink into himself, hoping he'd wake up different. He tried it on with me outside the Frolics bar below in Carney. I'd cycled out that far and was waiting for an offer of a spin home in a farmer's car. A ride for a ride; it's nearly biblical. I knew if I went with him it'd be the sorriest thing he ever did. I knew he was stone cracked about his wife. She was expecting at the time. I very nearly let him do it to me. I really wanted to. A few years later I'd have done it out of spite. But I pushed him off of me and belted him into the balls. I used to see him coming from Mass for years and years after that, with his wife and his two boys and his little girl. I don't think he knew me. I don't think he really saw me that time in Carney.

THERE'S PLENTY calls me a witch. It doesn't bother me. I haven't aged well; I look a lot older than I am. I have rheumatoid arthritis. It pains me everywhere. It has me curled over, balled up, all smallness and sharp edges. I'm like a cut cat half the time. Men never call here any more. My children never call to me, even. They're pure solid ashamed of me, after all I done for them. My daughters are beyond in England. My second fella, Hughie, is married to a strap of a wan that looks at me like she scraped me off of the sole of her shoe. They had a little girl I only seen once. Lord, my heart aches just to hold that child, blood of my blood. Millicent, they called her. Milly and Lily. Wouldn't it be lovely? My third boy is a solicitor in the city and my John-John is knocking around, never too far away, nor never too near.

He took a woeful set against me altogether, my John-John. The others just don't bother with me, but John-John arrives down the very odd time, roaring and shouting out of him, crying and shaking. He's gone to be a terror for the drink, anyway. His looks are leaving him; his face is getting puffed out and pasty-looking. It breaks my heart to see his lovely strong features crumbling away. I stand in the doorway and pull my cardigan tight around me. He shoves in past me sometimes, and takes what money does be in my jar on the top shelf over the fireplace. He doesn't know

I leave that money there especially for him. I expected too much from him; I know that. My John-John, my little man. I destroyed the boy by seeing too early the man inside in him. I think he thought he had to hate me to save himself.

I DO SEE that boy of the Mahons nearly every day, passing down the road to his father's house. I hear the spinning heart on their gate, creaking slowly around. The sound floats up along the road to me, waved along by the leaves of the trees. It puts me in mind of my own dry joints; my burning hip, my creaking knees. He's beautiful, that boy, tall and fair-haired, like his mother. His auld father is a horrible yoke. He got all his mother's goodness, that boy. He got no part of his father that I can see. Maybe there's something inside in him that he got from his father, but he keeps it well hid. He always salutes me as he passes; he waves and smiles and calls me by my name. Oh, he's solid gorgeous, so he is. I'd have married a boy like that if I hadn't been so busy going around being *wanton*, so determined not ever to be bound to a man.

I remember his mother well. She used to give me the time of day, not like a lot more around here who had themselves elevated in their own minds to heights far, far above me. A few of them are starting to fall from their heights, now. I see them in the village, shaking their heads at each other in disbelief, blaming everyone else. I don't know what she died of. I was fierce sad when I heard it. That boy was grown up at the time, but he came walking up the road looking like a small child, as pale as a ghost, with his eyes hollowed out from crying. He came into my kitchen that day and drank a sup of tea. Thanks Lily, thanks Lily, he kept saying. He'd fallen out with his mother, I knew that, but I didn't say anything to him, only that she was gone home now and he'd see her again some day. He was weak from sadness and regret, which is the most horrible feeling of all. I kissed him on the cheek before he left. I wished blessings for him, the poor love. He married a lovely girl after.

THERE'S SOMETHING unspeakable about the attraction between a man and a woman. It can't ever be explained. How is it that I could be so foolish for a big, fat mongrel of a man like Bernie McDermott? He did something to me whenever I saw him that made me weak in my body and mind. I wanted to please him more than I wanted to mind my children. I think if he'd asked me to throw one of them over the bridge and into the rushing weir, I'd nearly have done it. Except if it was John-John. I knew my last child was his from the first moment I felt him inside in me. He gave me hell from the start. I was up before the sun every morning, retching and crying and gasping for breath. I could hardly walk for nine months with the pains he caused me. My other children were pure solid neglected. Only for John-John they'd have melted away from the hunger and the dirt. Bernie McDermott never even noticed until I was the size of a house. Are you fuckin expecting? says he. I am, Bernie, says I. Fuck me, I thought you were just getting fat. How'll you figure out which of your mountain men is the daddy? Says I, it's you Bernie. Me? Ha ha ha! If you fell into a bed of nettles, how would you know which one stung you? I was with no one only you for near a year, I told him. He punched me into the stomach then, and pulled over the dresser in temper. All my crockery was smashed, and my lovely Child of Prague my mother gave me. John-John ran from the back room to protect me and Bernie McDermott slapped him right back across the floor and in through the door again. He came here no more bar the time he called to make ribbons of my face over naming him inside in the hospital.

They're big farmers, the McDermotts. Imagine if they knew there's a solicitor inside in the city, the son of a whore, who's kin of theirs. It'd frighten the life out of them to think of him with his brains *and* badness! He got the brains from me. I gave him the money to go in every day to the university. I got him all his books and the trendy clothes young fellas need to fit in. The day of his graduation, I stood outside the big building, squinting in through the glass, trying to see could I see him. Each student was gave two tickets for the ceremony. He gave them to his girlfriend and her mother. All I wanted was one look at him in his gown, with his scroll. One photograph would have done me, of him with his arm around me. I'd have had it blown up and framed and hung it in the porch, right in front of people's faces as they walked in. I was foolish to let pride into my heart. I still paid for him to finish off his studying above in Dublin, though. The little strap of a girlfriend and the auld mother who was never let see me was brought to *that* graduation too.

I LOVE all my children the same way a swallow loves the blue sky; I have no choice in the matter. Like the men that came to my door, nature overpowers me. I cry over them in the dark of night. I often wake up calling their names. I don't know why they all ran from me. I'll never be a burden to them. I know a concoction that will send me away into dreams from which I'll never wake. I've made it up already; I'll drink it back in one go when I can no longer keep a hold of my mind or body. There'll be no one sad after me, imagine. John-John will come out and take from the house what he can sell. And then he'll ollagoan below in Ciss

Brien's the way people will buy him drink in sympathy. Isn't that a fright, after a life spent blackening my soul for him, for all of them? Yerra what about it, sure wasn't I at least the author of my own tale? And if you can say that as you depart this world, you can say a lot.

Vasya

THERE IS no flatness in this land. It is all small hills and hidden valleys. Birds sing that I cannot see; they hide in trees and fly in covered skies. The horizon is close and small. There is daily rain that makes the earth green. Even in winter it is green. A short journey in any direction ends at the sea. I went one Sunday with a man I worked with and his family to the sea. I stood looking at the waves crashing on the beach for too long. I heard his child asking what I was doing. He hushed her. The man's wife scolded him for bringing me. She thought I couldn't understand. She was right and wrong: I didn't know the words, just their meaning.

In this country I speak in sentences of two words or three. I nod and smile often and I feel redness in my face when spoken to. When I worked each day on building sites, the foreman would point at things and ask with his eyebrows raised for understanding. I almost always knew then what to do. Their voices are fast. My mother's mother spoke that way, in a dialect of a tribe of reindeer herders from far north of my family's ground. She was full of wonder at our goats and cattle and horses. When we were children we would laugh at her strange, speeding tongue and my father would chase us from the camp. We would be banished to the fire's outer ring where the cold and heat battled. And still we'd laugh and my father would shout warnings from inside the camp. He was very fond of my mother's mother; he had travelled north to bring her to live with us when we received word of my grandfather's death.

The foreman's voice is soft and contradicts his appearance. He's younger than me but he reminds me of my father. The big work is gone now; many things are left unfinished. Some days of the month he asks me to help him to repair work that was done too quickly.

I'm called the Russian here, as almost everyone is from other countries. I don't mind. On the plain where I was born all of our faces looked the same to foreigners. The Latvians take offence and complain bitterly among themselves about slights best forgotten. The Russian and Polish men speak good English and try to explain the differences. No one here has heard of Khakassia. The Irish men laugh all day while they work and shout across the sites at each other in whooping voices. There was a man called Shawnee who would slap me on the shoulder and shout in a singsong voice and make the other men laugh. I would smile and look down at my work and feel my face becoming hot. I don't think he was being unkind.

Sometimes when I am in a good mood I act the fool. On the building sites I would ape the exclamations of the Irish. If I had difficulty with a tool or a machine I would put it down and stand up straight and shout CUNTOFAYOKE! The Irish men would look at me in mock astonishment and then look at each other and roar with laughter. GASMAN, they'd say, and shake their heads, laughing. I would feel happy, and then remember to be ashamed at myself for being a clown to please other men. I am too far from my father's home and from my brother's grave.

In the office where men and women go who have no work a girl asked me for a number, then for a stamp, then for the name of my employer. I could understand; I had heard all of these words before. Pokey Burke? She sighed. I looked at her in silence and shrugged. She rolled her eyes towards the ceiling. Then she smiled at me, but it was a smile that says I'm sorry. I didn't understand the next words she said, but her voice was kind. Shawnee whispered loudly and slowly from behind me while the girl looked at her computer screen: Hey Chief, what she's saying is you … don't … exist! And all the men and women in the lines laughed.

MY FATHER'S HERDS were small and spread across a plain and a sweeping valley. There was not enough to sustain all of us, so my brother and I journeyed south to a city that was spreading outwards like a dirty puddle. We lived in a hut of galvanized metal and scrap wood, near to where a great building was being erected. Its foundations were deeper than I thought even an ocean could be. I could not see their lowest part. My brother and I carried blocks to masons, along planks suspended above noth-ingness. We became braver each day and the other men began to respect us. You goatherds aren't bad, the boss said once. I felt pride and then foolishness. My brother must have misheard what the man had said and taken his words for an insult. He cast aside his burden and struck the man in the face. Other men, anxious to be in good favour with the boss, turned on my brother and kicked and beat him. I fought until blood ran down my face and into my eyes and mouth and my fists were raw and scorched with pain. My brother was almost unconscious when I dragged him clear of danger; there was a swelling on his forehead. I looked back from the street and the men that had attacked us were already turned away, bent once more to their labouring. The fat man my brother had struck was rubbing his chin, pointing and shouting orders.

My brother left our hut the next day and bought dirty vodka brewed by a man in a small still across the street, beaten together from a vat and a stolen distiller. He sang scraps of folk songs that night, half-remembered from our childhood. There was no music in his voice; he shouted and screamed the words and woke people from their sleep. Shut up Afanasiev, you fool, men said from inside their own shanties. No one had courage enough to stand before him, though. He staggered away from me as I reached for him to calm him and bring him inside; he fell, and pushed me away as I tried to help. The swelling on his forehead had not reduced. The next day, a local militiaman and a regular policeman came to our muddy street and began to ask for relatives of Viktor Afanasiev. He is my brother, I said. Your brother is dead, the policeman said. The militiaman had a stubby rifle slung around his neck. He stroked it as though it were a pet and said come with us. Viktor had been found lying in a gap between two buildings at the centre of the town. He'd been beaten again and had suffocated in blood. I could never return to my home without my brother.

I heard of men who were planning to travel to Western Europe. I asked them how this could be done and they gave me a piece of paper with names, addresses and numbers. That was four years ago. When I first reached Ireland I learned quickly how best to find employment. I took from others words and phrases that served me well for a while: *off the books, under the table, on the queue tee*. One man can learn some trades by watching another closely. I worked in two cities and then came to this village. There was work here and the air was sweet. I worked for Pokey Burke for nearly two years. Now I use the money I had saved for food and to pay my rent and I work some days for the foreman again. Bobby. He calls me the best of the 'see too' boys. I don't know what this means. I smile and nod.

I HAVE LEARNED the roads around this village. I know the way to a quay, on the edge of a lake of placid water. There are wooden seats at this quay to sit on and look at the water. The evening sun turns it to a glistening, dazzling thing that has no place on this dull earth except in that short time before sunset. That light is a trick: if I were to swim to it or row out to put my hand upon it, it would be gone as I approached and there would be only dark, cold water in its place. Across the bay there is another place, identical to the one where I sit. When the air is moist the distant bank becomes magnified and seems closer, as do the dark hills behind it. When the air is dry it moves away, and could be another country, across a sea. When it looks to be a distance that I could easily swim, I think of myself trying and of being seized halfway by a tightening of the muscles in my arms or legs. Or by the panic of the realization that I had misjudged the distance, that I had been tricked by the landscape and the light. No one on the shore would see that I was struggling; no one would hear me cry for help.

The road from the quay is steep and winding. Houses are hidden at the end of long avenues, lined with ancient trees, where I imagine families have lived, son after father, for years and years. These people are fixed, rooted, bound to a certain place. I think of my father's camp and the moving of the herds across thousands of miles of openness. I think of returning home, and how I would be a burden and a shame to my family. At the cattle station I would ask in which direction I must walk to reach my father's camp and the men there would ask, with disgust upon their faces, why I had returned. My father and mother would not embrace me. I'll stay here. I have the roads to walk and the clear air to breathe. I have the quiet lake and the light that dances on the water.

I walked once from the house where I live, before I had learned the way the roads lie and the way that this land can turn around on itself. I was tired of the men in the house; they were drinking and shouting through all the hours of the night and singing songs loudly of their different countries. A neighbour came to the door of the house and I heard him saying the baby, the baby. The other men quietened and became sullen. Without songs, they drank more deeply. I decided to walk towards the rising sun. I crossed the road, away from the rows of houses of light timber and thin blocks and entered a field ringed by trees. There was a river at the far side of the field. My eyes were deceived again and I walked into a wet hollow in the field's centre and over a small rise and then down towards the river. Cows were standing at the muddy edge, drinking. They were fat and contented, full to bursting, waiting to be milked. The grass here is thick and long. I envied them. I found a way across the river over rounded stones and climbed the shallow far bank. I kept true east across more fields and decided to make for the foothills of a small mountain where I had heard there was an old silver mine. I thought that by the time I had reached those hills and sat for a while and walked back that the other men would be asleep and I could have a Sunday afternoon of peace. I would make my food and drink tea and look for words that I knew on a newspaper.

I walked for hours and became lost. The fields dipped and rose and all looked alike. The hills seemed to draw no nearer. I came to a public house on a roadside. The Miner's Rest, it was called. Where is this place? I asked a man inside. Shallee, he said. I was walking, I am lost, I said in English. He seemed to understand my words. Where you from, boy? Khakassia, I said. Where the fuck is that? Siberia, I said. Jaysus friend, you sure are fuckin lost! And he roared with laughter and the others in the bar laughed as well and I don't know why but I felt at once safe and foolish and I laughed with them as they slapped my back. A man played a fiddle. He had a serious face but his music was full of joy.

At the next week's end, Pokey Burke gave me a lift to the house I shared. I had just finished shoring the foundations of a large house that would never be built. I have great time for you, he said, you're a fabbeless worker. I don't know what fabbeless is. I know I owe you a few bob, he said. I understood this. I'll sort you out next week, okay? Sort you out means pay you in this land. He looked at me and smiled as he drove. I knew he was lying. I knew I would not see him again. But I said okay, Pokey, okay, and I smiled back, and my stomach lurched as he drove too fast down into a valley that I didn't know was there.

Réaltín

THERE ARE forty-four houses in this estate. I live in number twenty-three. There's an old lady living in number forty. There's no one living in any of the other houses, just the ghosts of people who never existed. I'm stranded, she's abandoned. She never has visitors. I should go down to her, really. When Daddy and me went in to the auctioneers to ask about these houses, they let on they were nearly all sold. I wanted a corner house with a bigger garden, but the guy started fake-laughing, as if I was after asking for a solid gold toilet or something. He had at least half a jar of gel in his hair. I'll see what I can do, he said to my chest, in a martyred voice. He shook his head and sighed and said we'd have to pay the deposit that day. He said he couldn't promise us any of the houses would still be available the next day. I believed him, even though I should have known better. Daddy got all worried and flustered then, and drove like a madman back to the Credit Union to get me the cash. I'd love to go in to that auctioneer now and kick him in the balls.

Poor Daddy. He comes up here nearly every day. He walks up and down the rutted avenues. River Walk. Arra View. Ashdown Mews. He tuts and shakes his head at the boy racers' tyre tracks. He tries to pick up every fag butt and beer bottle. He looks in the gaping, empty windows; he scowls at the houses' spooky stone faces. He hums and whistles, and curses now and again. He slashes at weeds with his feet. He kicks at the devouring jungle. He's like an old, grumpy, lovely Cúchulainn, trying to fight back the tide. The only men in my life are my father and Dylan. It's not fair on them or me.

It was a few months before we copped on to what was after happening. The builder was gone bust. My house and the old lady's were the only ones he could finish, because we were the only ones who'd paid. We heard he'd put all his money into some stupid thing to do with a fake island or something out in Dubai. Now he's made a run for it. He's lucky, Daddy says, because if I ever get my hands on him I'll kick the living shit out of him. Daddy never talks like that. He must be really, really mad. Imagine if anything happened to him; I'd never get over it. Gaga, Dylan calls him. He stands at the sitting room window every morning, shouting Gaga, Gaga, Gaga. When he sees Daddy's car, he goes mad. He's a scream.

Daddy cuts the grass outside every house on this block. I watch him, sweating and steadfast, burning in the sun. He stops every now and again and stands behind his lawnmower with his head bowed. I wonder is he praying, or thinking about Mammy. Maybe he's crying. God, I hope he isn't. He says he does it to be doing something; he hates retirement. I know well he'd way prefer to be off playing golf. Or playing bridge with Bridget. He does it to make my life seem more normal, to see can he make the place look like a proper estate. He mows and strims and trims and puts all the cuttings into a trailer. Then he drives over to Cairnsfort Lodge, where the builder's parents live, and dumps the grass and stuff at the side of their garden. The builder's father says nothing. He wouldn't want to, Daddy says.

A camera crew came here a few weeks ago. They were making a documentary about ghost estates. They set up all their gear and knocked on my door and Daddy answered and he got really cross. There's no Dublin Four arsehole going using ye to make a name for himself, he said, when I went mad at him for not letting them interview me. I just wanted Dylan to be on telly, really, so everyone could see how gorgeous he is. Daddy wants us to go home and live with him and Bridget. I can't, though. Seanie would love that, for one thing; I can just imagine him in the pub with his stinky friends, saying she's gone back to her daddy, fwaah ha, with his big stupid donkey laugh. And I can't stand the way Bridget moves apologetically around the house, letting on she's not trying to replace Mammy. She's probably a nice person, but she can fuck off, to be perfectly honest. She wears that horrible, watery, flowery old-lady perfume. It smells like somebody took a bottle of okay perfume and poured out half the bottle and filled it up again with pee and then sprayed it all over her. She tries to talk to me about Daddy. I feel like screaming like a child at her to mind her own business, to leave me alone, to leave Daddy alone. When I don't engage she starts on about cards. Bridge. Forty-five. Whist. Jesus.

SEANIE CALLED UP last week. Hello Tom, he said to Daddy. Daddy only nodded at him, but he stopped mowing and followed him with his eyes up to the door. He came in with a bag of crappy plastic shit for Dylan. I let him stay for five minutes. Dylan smiled at him, the little turncoat. Daddy thinks Seanie is great, underneath it all. Would ye not try to make it up, love, he says. It kills Daddy not to be able to talk to him about hurling and cars and machinery and whatever men do be fascinated by when they're not ruining women's lives. Make it up? Make it *up*? We didn't have a *row*; I scream at poor Daddy, he's just *useless, useless, useless*. All he's good for is drinking and shagging *floozies*. Daddy starts looking at the ceiling and humming and scratching his chin. He tries to block my shrill, crazy voice from his poor old ears. He tries to keep my horrible words out. They settle around his heart and weigh it down. His blood quickens. His cheeks turn a livid purple.

Little star, my name means. Some star I am. I'm not sure if Seanie is even Dylan's father. Imagine if Daddy knew that! I had sex with my boss, George, just once. The horny old bastard brought us all out to celebrate his firm's thirtieth year. He said he was having a special do, just for us. Really, he was having a special do for himself, hoping and praying that if one of us girls got pissed enough, we'd start to think he was more debonair than wrinkled, more witty than embarrassing. I shouldn't ever drink. The old biddies all went home early; the apprentices took it easy of course, the cute arses – and I drank sticky-sweet fake champagne and laughed at every inane thing the creepy old pervert said. Two days later when I finally got over the nausea Hillary said that it was *so* obvious we were going to shag when he offered to share a taxi home with me. He got all business like afterwards, and wouldn't meet my eye. His willy was tiny, his balls were wrinkled and uneven. When I told Hillary that, she nearly choked on her rice cake. Dylan looks like nobody except my father. Thank God, thank God; he's the absolute image of Daddy.

George charged a flat rate of four grand for conveyancing all through the maddest part of the property boom. If you added up the hours of work for the average house purchase, and multiplied by our hourly rate, he could have made a good profit if he charged seven hundred. He never looked at those files, we did everything. George wasn't even the most expensive. A guy rang one day in a panic; the builders of some crappy estate had put his house back on the market. For some reason, George had his file in his office. The contracts hadn't been sent back in time, the builders were backing out of the original deal and wanted another ten thousand to go ahead. He sounded young. His voice was cracking and shaking. George was in court. The guy had to get the promise of ten grand off the Credit Union in the end. Those builders were chancing their arm, but I couldn't say that. I know now what I should have told him: tell the builders to piss off, stay in your flat with your girlfriend, wait two or three years and buy the same house for half the price. Hopefully he at least has other humans in *his* estate.

MY HEAD was all over the place. That's one phrase that I detest. It's a miserable excuse for doing miserable things. What does it even mean? I hear the scumbags saying it all the time in work, through George's door: Aw, my head was all over the place, I didn't *mean* to hit him with the iron bar, I would of never done it, only my brother was after been stabbed the night before and I knew in my *heart* and *soul* your man was fuckin goin round *skittin* over it …

The awful thing is, whenever I think of the way I was the time I was meeting Seanie and accidentally had sex with George, that's the phrase that comes to my mind. My head really *was* all over the place. Mammy wasn't long dead, and I'd never really grieved properly. I was so worried about Daddy, I just decided to block it out and focus on him. Then I realized I wasn't the only one focusing on Daddy; Bridget the bloodsucker was mooning about the edges of our lives, with her big sorry-for-you eyes and her weirdly perky old boobs. If I'm to be objective, I can't blame Daddy, though. Mammy was gone for years before she went. Next thing now my *special paid career break* will be over and I'll be back in work, listening to scumbags again and looking at George trying to not look at me, wishing I'd just go away again. What will I do with Dylan then? My mortgage is *half* my wages.

FOUR FELLAS came here in a van this morning. I thought they were Travellers first, coming looking for stuff to steal. They looked around for a while, hands in pockets, kicking stones like four lads trying to look innocent. They made me nervous; Daddy wasn't due for another hour or so. One of them was really good-looking, tall and fair-haired and weather-beaten in a lovely way. He caught me staring out at him; I made it worse by jumping back from the window. He came over to my door. The sensible-bitch side of me whispered the words *rape* and *murder* in my head, but I had to open the door before he rang the bell – Dylan was only halfway through his nap. Howaya, he said, ammmm … I shushed him; he looked embarrassed. I came out and closed the door behind me, as if to hide my lonely life. I was trying not to smile at him. Why am I such a fool for manly men? I pointed back with my thumb. Nap time, I told him. Oh, Jaysus sorry. No problem, I said, and let the smile have its way. He brightened a bit then. He said he used to work for the builder who built the estate. They were up checking if the C2 boys had been back to finish off. What the fuck is a C2 boy? He looked a bit shocked at my language. God, he must be a right delicate petal.

Self-employed workers, he explained, sub-contractors, foreign workers who were only taken on by builders if they registered as self-employed. That way the builder hadn't to pay the proper rates; stamps, tax, pensions or what have you.

His friends, a fat one, a foreign-looking one and a simple-looking one, were standing leaning against their van, trying to look like they weren't gawking over at us. I suddenly listed the things that were unfinished in *my* house, the loose skirting boards, the unpainted banister, the badly hung door, the wobbly kitchen tile, the lumpy garden, the missing fence panel. He wanted to know had I not gotten a snag-list done. A what? Another thing I should have known about. He sighed, then said he'd do all those jobs, *them* jobs, he said, but he'd have to charge, he didn't work for the builder any more. Forget it so, I said, I have zero money. Daddy had tried to do all of those jobs loads of times, but I'd never let him; I was foolishly insisting on waiting for the builder to come back. He looked over his shoulder at his friends and then back to me and said in a soft voice that he'd come back on Monday himself and do all the jobs. He'd charge fifty for labour and he'd probably be able to get any bits he needed from the other houses.

So now I have a whole weekend ahead of me of looking forward to Bobby the out-of-work builder coming to trudge around my house, dragging in muck around the place, putting Daddy's nose out of joint and probably frightening the life out of Dylan. I'll have to try and get into town tomorrow to buy a new top. How sad am I?

Timmy

I WALKED UP Fernley's Hill yesterday evening after I had my
supper ate. It was melting close so it was. I seen Bobby, but he
looked like he was right busy. He had a jeep and a trailer full of
blocks. He must've cut down a tree. I thought I heard chainsaws
a few nights ago all right. Rory Slattery was giving him a hand. I
seen his big fat head and it wedged up Bobby's arse. Seanie Shaper
always says if Bobby opened his mouth wide enough you'd be able
to see Rory Slattery looking out at you! I heard Rory is going away
to England soon to see about getting work in the buildings for the
Olympics. I'd say Bobby got a lend of the jeep and trailer off of the
Burkes. I wonder did he just go up and take it or did he ask Pokey's
father. I walked real slow all up along the road past Bobby's house.
His young fella seen me all right. He pointed over at me and went
Ti, Ti, Ti. I only waved at him. He knows my name on account
of I used always walk up there in the mornings to get a lift off of
Bobby if we were on a site I couldn't walk or cycle as far as. He

was standing in the garden, half the way between the fence and the front of the shed where Bobby and Rory were. They never seen me I don't think. I didn't go in to give a hand stacking the blocks. I kept walking up the hill and back down the far side and down the lake road and I thrown stones in the lake for a while and I skimmed one right good so I did. It bounced *five* times. That stuff always happens when there's no one to see it happening only yourself. Then you're not believed when you tell it.

A power of fellas is going foreign. I'm not. I might be asked to be a sacristan when Padjoe Ryan is dead I think. Father Cotter showed me the tabernacle one time and the press where the collection baskets do be. I'm fierce devoted to Our Lady so I am. Padjoe had a triple bypass a few years ago. There's so much copper pipes in him it's a plumber they'll have to get the next time he has a turn. That's what Nana said about him. Nana never got no copper pipes in her heart. She never went to a doctor once in her life either. Doctor me hole, she used to say. What the feck do they know about anything? All they do is pull and drag out of you and then send you in as far as the hospital to die. The hospital does be full of them auld black doctors. How's it them boys do be so worried about Irish people that they has to come over here to be doctors? Would they not look after all them starving babbies in their own places? And all them that's falling away dead of the Aids? That's what Nana used to say anyway. I don't know anything about it. Nana's heart just burst one night.

Nana used to be always saying how she lived her whole life only over the road a small bit from the house she was born in. She'd say aren't I as lucky as can be? There's not too many can say it, and a lot of them that can aren't happy over it. As if to say they've missed out on something in life by making their life in the place of their birth. I'd always agree away with her. Nana said this place has the best of all worlds. If you need something handy you can go in as far as the village on your bicycle, or you could walk it easily, or if you need something that can't be got in the village, there's three buses a day into town and they'll stop for you right at the gate. Nana often wondered to know why in the hell people get into years and years of debt for motorcars. Wouldn't one even do between two or three houses? Everyone does be going the same way anyway. That way the expense could be divided up and shared.

BOBBY WAS ALWAYS fair sound to me. He's the only one never slagged me. The first day I got the job off of Pokey, Mickey Briars who lamped me last year sent me in as far as Chadwicks for a packet of straight springs, a skirting ladder and a box of rubber nails. Your man in Chadwicks only laughed and shook his head and said I'd say your mates are pulling your leg. When I got back Mickey Briars was raging. He said years ago a fella starting off would've been sent all over the town from shop to shop for the joke messages the way everyone could have a go at laughing at him, and wouldn't you think the smart prick inside in Chadwicks woulda kept it up?

I'm glad he didn't all the same. I don't like the sound of getting made little of from pillar to post. Bobby laughed at that kind of a thing but he never really joined in with it. One time Seanie Shaper kept showing me pictures in a magazine of naked women and I didn't know what I was meant to do or say so I only smiled down at them naked paper women and all the rest thought it was a howl altogether and were asking to know had I a horn, and would they send me over as far as Lily the Bike and even the Polish and the Russian boys were roaring laughing at me and for a finish Bobby just walked over and grabbed the magazine off of Seanie and threw it into the fire in the tar barrel and said now, leave the boy alone to fuck. You yahoo. Seanie said nothing to Bobby. He was afraid of him when he was in a temper.

I got a woeful hop the day Mickey Briars went at me with the shovel. Bobby and them were hiding all in the yard while Mickey went tearing around, roaring and shouting out of him about how he was going killing Pokey and where was his fuckin money and all. I thought first it was all a mess because everyone that was hiding was roaring laughing and I didn't duck down behind a load of blocks like Seanie and Rory or climb up into the cab of a digger, only stood looking at auld Mickey as he ran at me. Bobby and them caught a hold of him and thrown him in the back of Seanie Shaper's van and Bobby gave me a hand to get up off of the ground and asked to know was I all right and I done my level best not to be crying like a baby but that's the sort of a battle I near always lose. I lid down that night after going home from the pub and the ceiling above me was spinning and spinning and I ran into the back toilet and got sick for ages. My stomach was burning and all. I'd say I was poisoned from the drink. I was quare lonesome that night, more even than all the other nights.

WE WAS ALL sent off different places when we were small. There was six of us in it. My father went stone mad on the drink when my mother died so he did. She died having me. I often do see him outside Ciss Brien's in the village or the Half Barrel inside in town, smoking a fag. He never says nothing to me. I do hate walking past him. My uncle took us all to the beach one time in a big van with windows. He drove to all the different houses we lived in to collect us: Nana's, Auntie Mary's, Uncle JJ's, his own house to get

Noreen, my big sister. Nana told me I was to bring her back a bag of seashells. I gave the whole day to finding shells for Nana. I went up and down the long beach a rake of times. Uncle Noely had to come and find me when it was time to go home. He was vexed over having to look for me. He grabbed me by the arm and dragged me up along the steps from the beach. My big bag of shells fell all over the path at the top. Noely wouldn't leave me pick them up. My bag was bursted anyway. I looked at them as we drove away from the beach. Seagulls were swooping down for a look to know were they something to eat that was after getting dropped. Then they'd fly off again, raging. Uncle Noely wanted to know why in the fuck was I crying over a few auld shells. I didn't know what to say to answer him. My brother Peadar laughed at me and gave me a puck. Nana gave out stink to Uncle Noely at home because I was burnt to a crisp. He never put no lotion on me.

Noreen had a baby who died after a few days. The doctor told her the baby wouldn't live after it was born. Noreen didn't believe it. She said the baby was beautiful, the baby was perfect, there was nothing wrong with the baby. The baby was brought home and all. All the nurses cried inside in the hospital as they left. They all knew well the little baby hadn't a hope in the world. Noreen wouldn't believe it, though. Sure look at him, Nana, look at him, he's perfect so he is, he's *perfect*. He was too, I seen him. There was something wrong with his heart; it wouldn't stay beating. I stayed close to Noreen's house the whole time after they brought him home so I did. I didn't like to be going in, tormenting them and they busy worrying and hoping and praying. I stayed outside in the shade of the big weeping willow that hung out over their wall. I let on to be standing guard against death. He got in, though, in spite of me. I heard Noreen from outside, roaring crying. PJ came out as far as the garden wall and called me in. Noreen had the little baby in her arms. She pulled me in to her arms as well. I couldn't hardly breathe with the flood of tears and the heat off of her and the little baby squashed into me. I knew you were outside the whole time, my love. I'm sorry, love, I'm sorry. I never minded you properly, love, and now aren't I paying for it? I'm sorry my little love, my little love, my little love. I didn't know for a finish was she talking about the baby or me. I think a lot about what Noreen said that day. I think she thinks it was my fault her baby died, like it was my fault Mammy died. I don't know in the hell.

WHAT WILL I DO for a job, I don't know? Imagine if Bobby went out on his own and gave me a job working for him! Jaysus, it'd be brilliant so it would. I'd work like a dog for him so I would. I have all the house painted below and I got a lend of a hedge trimmers off of Noreen's husband and done all the hedges up along the sides. I made a new panel for the back fence to replace the one that got blown down and busted up. I have every single weed pulled up from the roots the way they won't grow back. Nana would be delighted with me. My brother Peadar said I can go way and shite now if I think I'm having that cottage. He says we're all the same and equal in the eyes of the law when it comes to who owns the cottage. He says even if Nana wrote a will and left me the cottage, and she *didn't*, I'd have to pay a fortune in *inheritance tax*. You'd be a fine man now below in the Credit Union looking for thirty or forty grand with your no job and one arm as long as the other, Peadar says to me. There isn't a job to be got anywhere. Peadar wants Nana's house sold. He has to think of his own children, he says. He came down a few nights ago with a lad from the auctioneers. He had a right cool yoke that you have only to press against one wall inside in a room and it measures the whole room for you. It's like magic. *Lasers*, your man said, and winked at me. He was a sneaky-looking fucker.

You'd want to buck your ideas up, Peadar says. I'd love to say ah go way and have a shite for yourself. He'd probably go mad and puck the head off of me, though. He has a fierce short fuse so he does. Noreen told me I could live in their house. I don't want to; they might look at me and think of how their little baby was took off of them because Noreen didn't mind me. That's not true, but if it's what Noreen thinks, it's as true as it needs to be. I'd never upset Noreen. She's lovely, so she is.

I WENT IN as far as the new hotel in town because they rang me from the dole office to say I had to. I done an interview and all. Your man said it was for to be a kitchen porter. I'd have to wash the pots and stuff. It's a demanding position, your man said. He had a pink tie on him. Nana would've called him *a right-looking dipstick*. I couldn't stop looking at his pink tie. He showed me the place where I'd have to wash the pots and all. There was a foreign fella inside in it; he was bent over a big sink, scrubbing like mad. His britches was drownded wet and all. He looked at me as much as to say he'd slit my fuckin throat for me if I went near his potwash. Some of them foreign boys do have a fierce dark eye. Your man with the pink tie asked to know who was my referee. I looked at him with my mouth open until he asked who could he ring for a *reference*. Oh ya, Bobby Mahon, I said. Is he a former employer? Ya, I said. Then No. Ya. No. Ya. Sort of.

Jesus Christ, your man said and shook his head. Look, I'll let you know.

He will I'd say.

Brian

I REMEMBER the mother and father talking about Matty Cummins and the two Walshes and Anselm Grogan and all them boys when they went to Australia a few years ago. A right shower of wasters they called them. Imagine fecking off to the far side of the world to drink their foolish heads off and the power of work to be had here! Context is everything. Pawsy Rogers used to be always saying that. Context is the first thing to examine in a statement. Aboy Pawsy, you were bang on on that score, boy. I'm fecking off to Australia now, and my mother keeps crying and my father won't talk about it. He's in denial. (He reckons if he doesn't acknowledge something, it doesn't really exist, like gayness, drugs or Marilyn Manson. When they were all on about Donal Óg coming out of the closet below in Cork, the father would only hum and look out the window when anyone mentioned it. Jaysus, what about your man of the Cusacks, Paddy? Dee dee dee dee ...)

So I'm going to Australia in the context of a severe recession, and therefore I am not a yahoo or a waster, but a tragic figure, a modern incarnation of the poor tenant farmer, laid low by famine, cast from his smallholding by the Gombeen Man, forced to choose between the coffin ship and the grave. Matty Cummins and the boys were blackguards; I am a victim. They all left good jobs to go off and act the jackass below in Australia; I haven't worked since I finished my apprenticeship. He has to go to the far side of the planet to get work, imagine, the mother does be saying to her ICA crowd. How is it at all we left them run the country to rack and ruin? How's it we swallowed all them lies? You can be certain sure there's no sons of *bankers* or *developers* or *government ministers* has to go off over there to get work. After all the trouble we had to get him through his exams and all.

What trouble? It was I had to do the bloody things. Boo hoo hoo, like. And the da's eyes glaze over and he starts to suck his false teeth and squint out the window at nothing if anyone mentions it. If I was leaving a good job to go, he'd be every day telling me I was a yahoo and a blackguard and getting right thick. I could cope with that a lot easier. At least I could tell him to shut the fuck up and we could have a row and I could feel anger instead of guilt. I can't tell him shut up if he says nothing. I wouldn't say he even *knows* he's humming.

I was only ever thinking about going to Australia because every single person I know went over there for at least a year and had unreal craic. Could the parents not just get over it, like? Jaysus, you'd think I was going to Afghanistan to take on the Taliban. I heard the mother giving out stink to the father about it the other night; she was doing the old shout-whisper: He's too *young*, Paddy, he'll drink his *head* off and spend all his money trying to keep up with the boy of the Farrells and he'll get no *job* or *anything*. He won't ever go to *Mass* out there, you can be certain sure. The Aussies is all turning against the Irish, too – didn't they kick a crathur to *death* outside a pub over there only a few months ago? Dee dee dee dee, the father said. She was fairly torturing him. Paddy, will you talk to him about it? Will you tell him it doesn't matter about the ticket, sure what about it if he loses the money, we'll put it back in his Credit Union for him, Paddy, will you Paddy, will you? *Paddy?* Doo doo doo doo ...

My young wan broke it off with me two weeks ago. She said there's no way she's going to have me riding all around me below in Australia while she waits here like a fool. She seen the lads' Facebooks; in every single photo they were pawing girls in bikinis. Forget that, she said. Then she started looking at me really closely, and sort of laughing nervously, and asking was I crying. Are you *crying*? Jesus Bri, are you actually *crying*? I was in my hole. Dopey bitch. As if I'd cry over her. *She'll* be crying the next time she sees me; I'll have got rid of the belly, I'll have an unreal tan, and I'll be home for a visit only before heading back out to my beach house and my job making four or five grand a week. Slapper. Is that it so, she wanted to know as I put my runners back on, are you just going to go? Have you nothing to say to me? I hadn't. I kicked her bedroom door before I left, though. JESUS, she went. Then I met her auld fella on the stairs, with his big manky tacher like Joseph fucking Stalin and his little beady eyes full of suspicion. I should have gave him a slap. Bollocks.

You know the way you get used to getting the ride? And then you're cut off, like, all of a sudden? That's what all them wankers do be feeling when they're going around crying over women. They're only missing the ride. Love is a physical mechanism that ensures humanity's survival. It's an abstract concept as well, for people to write songs and books and make films about. Either way, it's nothing but a *construct*. That's the kind of auld shite I used to write in English. Pawsy used to cream himself over it. You have a keen mind, Brian. I do, ya. In me hole. You should look at arts or humanities, Brian. Avoid construction, Brian. Don't be tempted by the high wages, Brian, they won't last. Don't waste your *brain*, Brian. All right, Pawsy, leave it go, in the name of all that's good and holy, let it go.

I won't think about Lorna again after I start tapping some fine blondie wan below in Australia, that's what I'm getting at. It's only the want of a ride is making me all emotional at the moment. That's the pervasive influence of popular culture: I *think* I'm sad over Lorna. It's all this shite on MTV. On an intellectual level, I couldn't give a shite about her. It's a strange dichotomy, so it is; feeling and knowing; the feeling feels truer than the knowing of its falseness. Jaysus, I should write this shite down and send it to Pawsy before I go.

Kenny came over earlier. He has a load of Es bought, and we heading off in less than a week. He's some spa. We'll be off our heads all week youssir, he says, we won't hear the auld wans bullshitting. Kenny is afraid of his shite of the flight; I know well. He's also afraid of upsetting his parents. We're all afraid of our lives of upsetting our parents. Why is it at all? Why have we to be bound by this fear of the feelings of others? Is it because my actions will always affect them? Am I the anti-matter particle to their matter particle, always having a direct effect on each other, even with a galaxy between us? Will the Earth's largest ocean be deep enough to drown my guilt? Whoo boy, I have to stop thinking. I'll be writing in a diary next, like a right prick.

I know for a fact now it's going to be a big huge ordeal going to the airport. The mother will want to come. She'll mither the whole way. She'll roar and scream at the father. He'll drive along at about forty, hunched over the wheel, knuckles white, teeth gritted. If I see him crying, I'll start crying too. Kenny will snigger and slag me the whole way to Australia. He'll probably find the sexiest airhostess to tell all about it. Well gorgeous! Hey, you should a seen this lad the whole way to Shannon! Crying like a child! Will you give him a lend of your make-up there hey, it might fuckin cheer him up a bit! Fwahahahaaaa! Put on a bleedin chickflick for him there, hey! Fwahahaha! Sometimes I'd love to box Kenny in the face. But I'm getting thick over things he *might* say, which is a tad unfair on the chap, in all fairness. I'm living on my nerves. I'm like a young wan on a heavy period. Let me out of here, for Christ's sake.

I SAW Bobby Mahon this morning, over beyond at the Height. I was up with the da, pulling weeds and letting on to be praying for the souls of the Faithful Departed. I might as well humour him another while, in fairness. Bobby was coming over the stile beside the locked gate as we came to it. He's meant to be tapping a flaker of a wan from town that used to go with Seanie Shaper that bought one of the houses in Pokey Burke's estate of horrors. There's war over it. You should see his wife as well, your wan Triona — she's a ride and a half. Bobby is a pure bull, though, so he is. He probably rides the two of them every day. Things come easy to guys like Bobby Mahon. He's not the brightest star in the firmament, but he's a proper man. He has nothing to prove. Kenny reckons he's like Paul Newman in *Cool Hand Luke*; no fucker could break him. He wore his hurley off of the McDonaghs' full forward at the end of The County Final We Nearly Won. Then he flung it away and lamped five or six fellas before Jim Gildea the sergeant and about twelve other bollockses got between him and the McDonaghs' boys. I was only a small boy at the time. I wanted to be Bobby Mahon. I still do, imagine. I'm some loser. Why can't I want to be me?

Trevor

I'M NOT SURE what time Mother gets up. I'm always gone before she stirs. I drive as far as Galway some days. I still get scared crossing the bridge in Portumna, like I used to as a child. The planks on the wooden stretch still clank loosely, as though they could break under the car. On a sunny day in Eyre Square you can sit and look at girls' legs all day long. Some of those girls wear skirts so short you can almost see their underwear. I bought a pair of sunglasses that block the sides of my eyes so that they can't see me looking at them. The trick is not to let your head move as you follow them with your eyes. I tried to hide my wraparound shades from Mother. She found them, though; she must have been rooting around in my car. She asked me what I was doing with them. She said they were plastic rubbish. She said she hoped I didn't wear them going through the village. She said people would think I was gone mad. She said I'd look a show wearing those things. She looked at me and shook her head. I didn't know what to say, so I just looked at the ground. I saw her putting my shades into the pocket of her apron.

I'm dying. I'm sure of it. One day soon my heart will just stop dead. I sometimes have a striking pain in my left hand. It could be a blockage in an artery. Sometimes I feel light-headed, sometimes I feel a pounding in my temples; my blood speeds and slows, speeds and slows. Last night, just as I was drifting off to sleep, I started violently. My heart must have stopped and then kick-started itself again. I'll die soon. I hope I don't know it's coming; I hope I'm asleep. I hope my lungs don't constrict and burn for want of air. I hope my brain doesn't show me scary pictures as it shuts down. I hope my life isn't concentrated into seconds and flashed across my consciousness like a scream. I hope I just stop.

I saw that girl again yesterday afternoon. She was standing outside her house, watching a child playing on a plastic tractor. The child was shouting, loudly and almost absentmindedly; long shouts with a rising note at the end. He looked like he was two and a half or maybe three at the oldest. He looked happy. Her house is painted white and there are flowers planted in the borders of her small front garden. It's like one good tooth in a row of decaying ones. Mother's friend Dorothy lives in the only other house that's occupied in that estate. She seems to think I'm her houseboy. Mother says she paid through the nose for that house, way more even than the market value at the time. She was desperate to downsize from her draughty old lodge. She got rightly stuck above in that place, Mother says. She thought she'd be right swanky!

Dorothy asked me to paint her window sills last week. I came on Saturday with white paint and a brush. I brought a flat-head screwdriver to open the tin. That's not emulsion, she screeched at me. You need *emulsion*. I imagined myself plunging the screw-driver into one of her milky eyes. Would she die straight away, I wonder? Maybe she'd spin and scream and claw at the protruding screwdriver. A fine mist of blood would spray in a widening arc as she spun. The blood would be pink, full of oxygen. That girl might run down to see what was going on. Dorothy would have finished gurning by then. You *killed* her, she'd say. I had to, I'd tell her. She wasn't really a human. She was a vampire. Dorothy would explode into dust, then. And that girl would rush into my arms.

I FEEL a pain in my lower back lately, if I stand still for too long. The pain travels around to the front sometimes. It could be my kidneys failing, shutting down, stopping. It could be testic-ular cancer, too. The pain from that often manifests in dispa-rate body parts; it can travel down your leg, up your spine, into your stomach. I could be riddled with tumours. I probably am. I definitely have skin cancer. Mother never used sun block on me when I was a child. She murdered me when I was a child by giving me skin cancer. A slow, undetectable murder, a pre-emptive strike, a perfect crime. She's a genius, the way she makes evil seem so normal. She can be evil while making a cake, without even blinking. She flaps around in a cloud of flour so that her sharp old head seems to float, disembodied, above it, and says things like: What were you doing for so long in the bathroom? Or: Dorothy's son is a *captain* in the army now, you know. Or: Who ever heard of a young *man* with a certificate in Montessori teaching? Or: You're gone as fat as a fool.

    Sometimes I just catch a glimpse of her black, forked tongue as it flicks back in. I wonder if she knows I've seen it. I think she thinks I see it but don't believe it to be real. I think she thinks

I think I'm going mad. She's trying to drive me mad. These creatures feed on madness, obviously. Dorothy is one as well. I could easily just kill them both, but I need a way of making sure everyone knows what they are before I move against them. If I just kill them, I'll be sent away to prison, or to the Central Mental Hospital in Dundrum if I plead insanity. If I kill them and expose them for what they are, I'll be a hero. They smell the same; they look more or less the same; they are concomitant in evil. I'm going to have to take that child from the girl who lives near Dorothy. Lloyd will help me. I won't let Lloyd hurt him or anything. We probably will have to put some marks on him, though. Then I'll kill Mother and Dorothy and tell everyone that I apprehended them just as they were about to sacrifice the child. They're witches, I'll say. They've held me prisoner with a spell since I was a baby. Don't touch their bodies, I'll say, they may not be really dead. The authorities might require my services as a consultant. I am probably the only living soul who knows how to spot these creatures and deal with them.

SOMETIMES I sit and think for hours about things. And then I fall into a sort of a reverie. After the reverie abates, I don't remember what I was thinking about before it, I just know that I was thinking too hard. My head pounds dully. It happened last evening, while I was sitting on the couch, watching through the kitchen door as Mother baked a cake. After it, I was slumped forward. My head was almost resting on my knees. *Judge Judy* was nearly over. Mother was shaking me. I had a strange picture in my head of Mother with a forked snake's tongue. Trevor, Trevor, oh Trevor, she was saying as she shook me awake. Her eyes were wet with tears. I'm okay, Mother, I told her. You're not, she said, you're not okay at all. We'll have to send you over to Doctor Lonergan. You'll have to get something to keep you together. I couldn't bear it if you fell to pieces the way your father did.

My father split in two, and then fell to pieces. That's what I think schizophrenia is: splitting in two and then falling to pieces. Am I a schizophrenic? Is it hereditary? I could find out, but I don't want to. Like I needed only to open the wardrobe door to find out if there was a monster waiting in there to kill me, but I never did. I might have woken him if I did. I'm not waking a monster. No way.

I WONDER if that girl that lives near Dorothy has a boyfriend. She has no husband anyway, Dorothy says. Dorothy obsesses about her. Three different men call to her. A scruffy-looking character who seems to be the child's father; he takes him walking by the hand up and down the road. An older man who must be her father. He mows grass all up and down her road. He tidies up that whole road by himself. He's a respectable-looking man, too, Dorothy says, very straight-backed and just handsome enough to not be too aware of it. He must be pure solid ashamed of that one, Dorothy says, with her brazen chest and her bastard child. And a tall, fair-haired chap with muscles and sunburn started to call to her a few weeks ago. He's called at least three times now. He marches in and out with tools and pieces of wood. He could be just doing jobs for her, Dorothy says, but they're very *familiar* with each other. She always *touches* him. There's no knowing what way she pays him for his work. She has no job, that one. She probably was given that house by the County Council. Imagine that, Dorothy says, you get rewarded handsomely these days for being a little hussy!

I'm going to paint Dorothy's window sills very, very slowly indeed. I need to see this tall, sunburnt, muscle-bound person for myself. I need to know what kind of relationship he has with the girl. He is a bogey, an unknown quantity. I can't think of her without him creeping into my mind's eye. She was wearing a denim skirt one day. Does he put a big, rough hand up her skirt? I'd like to think he is respectful of her, but there aren't many respectful men in the world. He probably asks her to do things for him and she feels she has no choice, because she is afraid he won't finish the jobs he has started. That's what those fellows are like. I would have to intervene if I happened to see him forcing himself on her while I painted Dorothy's upstairs window sills. I would kick in her front door and he'd turn towards me and I'd hit him with the heel of my hand full force into his solar plexus, killing him instantly. It's okay, I'd tell the girl, while she sobbed in my arms. It's okay, the monster is gone, the monster is gone. I hope my heart doesn't stop before I get to save that girl. I don't feel very well. I think I've been thinking too hard again.

Bridie

I ALWAYS SWORE I'd never again set foot in County Clare. I don't even like to look across at east Clare from the low shore at Castlelough. Ton Tenna mocks me from the Limerick road: it hides Clare behind it. We had a meal in a lovely restaurant in Ballina one time, but I kept my back to the river, because Clare was on the far bank. My second son went fishing with his uncle Jim and his brothers in Clare nearly twenty years ago and was swept off of a rock and drowned. I can't bear the thought of that county since. I think every hour of every day about him still. I think mostly about the last moments of his little life: the shock he must have got when the wave grabbed him; the way he must have felt as he was dragged out and out and under. Could he hear the roars of Jim and his brothers? Could he feel the ocean tightening its hand around him? I know I shouldn't think these things over and over again, but you may as well ask a bee to leave the flowers alone.

The day it happened, our neighbour John English drove us out as far as Spanish Point where the search party was organized. I'll never forget that drive; the last time I had hope. There were no mobile phones that time, so I kept thinking we'll get there now and they'll have him, wrapped in thick white towels, shivering and crying from the shock and the cold. If there had been a longer road, I'd have made John English take it. I'd have stayed in that car forever, safe with hope. I knew the minute we pulled up there was no hope for my boy – no one seemed to be *hurrying*. I screamed at them all to get back into the sea, to hurry, hurry, he'll be halfway to America, but they only looked sadly at me and then out at the rolling blue and shook their heads. He was never got for a finish. The greedy Atlantic ate him and kept his little bones.

I charged like a madwoman off up along the coast road towards Quilty for miles and miles that day, looking out at the ocean, as if I might spot him, treading water and waving his little hand, waiting to be rescued. There was a second search party raised to find *me*. I came to a little church with a lovely name: Star of the Sea. I went in and knelt down and blessed myself and bowed my head and anyone looking on would have thought I was praying to God for my lost son. I wasn't, I was cursing Him. You bastard, I was saying, you bastard, just because *your* son was killed, have we all to suffer forever? Have you not had enough revenge? And your boy only stayed dead three days. Will *my* boy be back on Sunday, the way yours was? I never went to Mass again. I stayed away from God and Clare for twenty years. Now I'm thinking of going to *live* in Clare, and not that far from where Peter was lost, in a new hotel as a live-in housekeeper. I'd be *head* of housekeeping, actually, if you don't mind.

My husband blamed me for Peter's death. It was *my* brother took him off fishing. It was *I* left him off that day with his little shorts on him, slathered with sun-cream, with his rod and his bag of sandwiches and sweets, hardly able to talk with the excitement of being allowed go fishing in the sea with his uncle and his brothers. If *he'd* been there, Michael said, he'd have warned him of the dangers, he'd have had my brother well told not to take his eyes off him for a second, he'd have done the world of things I didn't do. The list of things he'd have done got longer and bigger over the years until we couldn't see each other at either side of it, and he left and never came back and the only difference was the noise of him was gone. There was no more and no less pain. We pass each other every now and again; we only barely nod. The children don't tell me what they talk about with him. I don't care. He's gone very old-looking lately.

I HAVEN'T A penny left. Michael sent money every single week until the last one left home, and then the envelopes stopped. I worked for years and years below in Thurles in the Town End Hotel. I was let go last year and they gave my job to a skinny little young wan. I went in and said it to Mary Wills, the personnel manager. Oh, that wasn't *your* job we gave that girl, Bridie, you were never a *manager* you see, she's been taken on as an accommodation *manager*. It would have been against the law to make me redundant and then to give someone else my job, so they made up a new name for my job and gave it to that little strap. Next thing didn't I see an ad in the paper for interviews for jobs in a new hotel that was opening. Anyone could go, all you had to do was go in as far as Nenagh to the Abbey Court and wait your turn to talk to some little madam in a short skirt who thought she knew it all. Your CV isn't very *varied* Bridie, she smirked at me. I haven't had a very varied life, I told her. I never missed a day of work though, or looked for a rise, or left a speck of dirt in a room. I didn't even want their poxy job, but I have it got now, and the offer of living in and having all my meals there. You could get a lot worse offered to you in this day and age. In the *current climate* as the fella says.

I told my second-youngest fella I was thinking of selling the house. You should have seen the way his face fell. He's shacked up inside in town with a *doctor's* daughter, if you don't mind. She's studying for her Master's inside in the university. He's studying his options, thank you very much. I'd give him two options: a kick in the hole or a kick in the hole. He's too used to being able to swagger in here, dragging in all sorts of muck and germs, with a puss on him like a slapped arse every time he fights with that wan. She was here one time. He's so *sensitive*, Missus Connors. He is, I said, he's a delicate little flower all right. She smoked fags into my face and looked down her nose at my house, and got the world of ash on my lovely clean carpet even though I actually put an ashtray on her *lap*. She hadn't a pick on her. She doesn't eat meat. Neither does Eugene, now. He says it isn't natural for humans to eat the flesh of other animals. It's an *evolutionary aberration*, he says. I'll give him an aberration into the mouth one of these days. If you saw the way he used to eat my roast beef – he hardly used to use a fork.

Isn't it a fright the way I get risen like that, so easily? And the poor boy still only feeling his way around the world. Sure, he hasn't a clue how clueless he is. God help us, he's still a child. I'm the same way with all of them: I can take the faces off of them with only the very slightest provocation. I changed when the sea took my Peter. I was never short-tempered or judgmental before it happened. I always encouraged people and forgave easily and laughed troubles away. But for years and years after it happened

I used to hear them in the next room, my children, huddled together, whispering nervously, the odd stifled giggle breaking the gloom, while I stomped around the house, shouting about nothing, about everything, about dust and dirt and dishes and attitudes and how none of them ever did a hand's turn to help in the house and how it was a fright to God to say I had a big family and still and all I was left alone in the world. Then one day there was no more huddles in the front room and no more nervous whispering; they were all gone, as fast as their legs could carry them. They'd sooner pay sky-high rents inside in the city for little boxes of mouldy apartments than have me every day stripping the good out of their lives, ruining their fun, blocking their sun.

I couldn't ever get over it. I was never able to get around it. I never forgave my brother or my sons that were there that day or God or the sea or the wind. I never forgave myself. I could never get the light to go back on in my mind. I never found peace. I told John Cotter to go way and fuck off for himself one time. There aren't too many have actually said that to a priest in spite of all the auld bile you hear people spouting these days. He got an awful shock: he'd been sitting there, in my house, talking gently the way he does, with those lovely words that most people would let rub gently against their wounded hearts, but I could only feel the anger building and building inside me until I knocked my tea off of the arm of my chair on purpose, I slapped it clean across the good room, and he jumped and looked at me and he must have seen the devil looking back at him because his face dropped and he hopped up from his chair and I told him where to go and where to shove his Scriptures and Michael rushed into the room and started apologizing and sure I blew the lid completely then and screamed and roared that no fucker had apologized to *me*, and I screamed on and on and on and there was no quieting me.

I SAW that girl of the Cahills that married that boy of the Mahons below in the post office on Thursday. Triona, her name is. She had their little boy with them. He's the pure solid cut head off of his father. He's solid gorgeous. She looked wretched. She was three or four ahead of me in the queue. The queue wraps around in an S, so the coven of auld bitches that are forever standing in that queue got a fine view of her. They'd look at her and then look back at each other with mock sympathy, their eyes glistening with delight, with triumph. The whole place has it that Bobby is doing a line with a little strap of a wan from town that bought one of Pokey Burke's houses. Ha ha, them auld biddies are thinking, that shook her! I wonder is it true. I normally wouldn't care a bit; only that Bobby is a lovely boy. I'd hate to think he was just a rotten auld faithless yoke like so many more. There's something in that boy; the way he looks at you while he's talking, sort of embarrassed so that you nearly want to hug him, and with a distance in his eyes even when he's looking straight at you, that makes you think there's a fierce sadness and a kind of a rare goodness in him. So, if that boy is off doing a line with some little piece of fluff I'll eat my hat. Maybe it's because I always think of him the day of his mother's funeral, and he fully grown at the time but still and all he had the eyes and the expression of a small boy and to look at him that day, anyone else bar me would have asked God for some of his pain so he hadn't to bear it all alone. I was out with God though, for good and glory, and was finished asking Him for anything.

I went mad doing things to the house one time. Michael didn't argue. The drilling and hammering drowned out the sound of me, I suppose. We got a delivery of blocks early one morning, for the bottom wall of a sunroom we were putting up at the back of the house, stretching into the garden. Michael wanted to be certain sure the lorry wouldn't be spotted by too many, the way there wouldn't be too much auld talk out of the neighbours about planning permission or what have you. You'd never know what way people are going to react to changes in their surroundings or to a bit being gone from their view of a field they never looked at in the first place. But we were spotted taking in our blocks anyway: Frank Mahon walked down along past us just as the two boys in the lorry were jumping down out of it. He had an auld scraggy-looking yoke of a dog with him and it collared with a piece of twine and a bolt or something shoved in through the knot so as to stop the poor creature from being choked by a tightening of it if he pulled against the mean twine too hard.

This was a fair few years ago now and that man's wife wasn't long dead. And there I was, and Michael only a step or two behind me, and the only noise to be heard was a ticking from the lorry as the heat left it. I can hardly think of words to describe what I saw, or the strange feeling of it. Frank Mahon stopped across from our gate, against the far ditch and stood looking up along the gable end of our house. And I suddenly knew why: one of the two boys doing the delivery was Bobby, his son. The world and his wife knew those two had had a big falling out.

Bobby was facing me, coming in the gate. His mate was foostering with the controls on a panel attached to the lorry's flat bed. And Frank was standing still, looking across, and it was for all the world as though Bobby sensed him there and he froze. And he couldn't have known he was going to be there; they'd arrived at our gate from opposite directions. I saw with my own eyes the colour draining from that boy's cheeks. His face never changed, but I swear a sadness you could nearly touch came down over it, and he turned slowly. There was nothing said for long seconds, and Michael and myself stood rooted to the spot. And then Bobby Mahon said: Well Dad.

Just that. Well Dad. And his father just stood looking at him and his eyes were an ordinary blue like any man's but still and all, as dark as night. And he raised his arm and pointed across at his son with the bit of a sapling stick he had in his hand and it was like as if a cloud had darkened the sky, even though the early-morning light never changed. And he lowered his arm and opened his mouth as if to say something. God bless us, said Michael under his breath, as if he couldn't help it. Howya Frank! And the cold spell was broken as auld Frankie Mahon turned away and walked off down the road towards the village, away from his pale son. That all took only a handful of seconds but I felt after it as though the entire morning was gone.

Bobby wouldn't even take a few bob for himself off me that day, for doing us that turn. I think maybe he remembered the time when he was a child that he and his mother gave a whole day and night in my house when his father was gone mad on the drink and was after making splinters of every stick of furniture that was in their little cottage below. I met them on the road, she was crying and he was barefoot. I picked them up and brought them home and asked her nothing. I didn't embarrass her. She was graceful and quietly grateful; she knew I knew he was below, wrecking the place. We'd have been great friends after, I'd say, if my little Peter hadn't left this world and taken my heart and soul with him. How is it at all that I let one child take my whole heart? It wasn't fair on anyone. Life isn't fair, as the fella says. He can say that again.

Jason

I SEEN a lad walking up the road towards me that day last week when your man Bobby Mahon killed his father. But then the lad hopped in over a wall before I could make out who it was. The dogs smelt something. I know in my heart and soul it was Bobby Mahon. The dogs smelt death. We walked on down past Bobby Mahon's auld lad's cottage and he was dead inside in it and we never knew. I seen him just after he done it. He must of still had blood on his hands. I wish now I would of gotten them glasses that time they was free on the Social besides going around squinting like a fool. I seen him again on the news being taken in to be charged, handcuffed to a big fat cop. Some lads do try to cover their faces when they're getting taken in and out of court. Bobby looked straight into the camera and there was nothing in his face. It *must* have been Bobby I seen that night last week. I wonder is there any gain to be had in telling the cops what I seen. I have no problem telling the cops stuff about a lad that'd do his own father in. Fuck him. Why wouldn't I? They might be a bit slower to stick their big red noses into my business the next time if I put the bollocks in the right place at the right time for them. Fuck it, though, I won't I'd say. He's a sound skin all the same.

THE BIGGEST MISTAKE I made when I was younger was getting tattoos all over my face. The very minute you've a tattoo on your face, the whole world looks at you different, even if it's a real nice tattoo, like birds or flowers or something. I done it for a woman. I only had a few birds up my neck that time. She told me I'd look rapid with a spider on my cheek. I would've done anything she wanted. She was sixteen and I was eighteen but she had way more brains than me. She had it all worked out and wrote down on a sheet of paper how much she could claim for this and that and the other and she even had it worked out how much she could get with one child, two children, three children and so on down the page. She knew *everything*. She had her life all planned out. All she needed off of me was a bareback ride. After I done the business she only wanted to have a laugh off me till the next prick came along. I only ever seen my young fella once. He was mad-looking. She was gone right fat but I'd still of rode her in a flash. I wonder how many has she now.

My mother and father got the house out here on account of me being a dependent adult child. My head is all over the place since I was small on account of I was fiddled with by a fat nonce down the road from our old house inside in town. He used to put on videos of all the films my auld fella never took me to see and I'd come in and watch them like a fool and he'd stick his hand down my pants while I stood there, eating my ten-pence bars, glued to the fucking *Ninja Turtles* or *The Lion King* or some shite.

I was diagnosed with post-traumatic shock, attention deficit hyper-activity disorder, manic depression, scoliosis, psoriasis, addictive personality and a few more things. I learnt them ones off by heart for telling them shitbags inside in the welfare office where to stick their fuckin job interviews. Here, Jason, go out there to Dell for an interview. I will in my bollocks, I have … and then I'd list off all my things wrong with me and eventually the shitbag would get sick of my bullshit and say okay, okay, for fuck's sake, just sign on so to fuck. All you have to do is start interfering with them cunts' tea breaks and they'll do anything to get you to fuck off.

I got the post-traumatic shock years ago after this mad auld culchie shot a lad right in front of me. The lad that got shot nearly died and all – they had to cut his leg off. My head was in bits after that for ages. He would of shot me too I'd say only he was using a shotgun and when his two shots was gone he thrown the gun in over a wall and fucked off. I think he thought we gave some friend of his a hiding or something. I nearly shat in my pants when he shot your man Eugene. I thought fuck this; I'm a dead man. I was paralysed with the fear, man, I don't mind telling you. I might have pissed a small bit in my pants, even. I don't think anyone noticed though, I had a white tracksuit legs on me. The mad auld bollocks went off then and done away with himself and the whole lot. That just shows he knew he was in the wrong. I never went near nobody. I might have kicked some farmer lad in the face a few times but he was a smart cunt who always gave your man Eugene a load of shit in school and all. I didn't want nothing to do with these culchie boys' feuds but it seemed only decent to help that Eugene prick seeing as he was so upset over your man. And he was a sound skin, that Eugene; he was my only pal out in this hole. I bursted my tackie off of your man's head and the whole lot.

I didn't stop at the spider on my cheek. I was in a bad way over that wan that had a child for me and then slammed the door of her brand-new apartment in my face. I didn't want the spider reminding me of her the whole time so I got it turned into a sort of a fat Celtic cross, but it ended up taking up nearly a whole half of my face and then I looked unbalanced only having shit on the one side so your man done a snake up the other side, sort of looking over at the cross with its tongue sticking out. It looked rapid at the start but now I think my face must've gotten fat because the snake is all wavy in the wrong way and flat and crappy-looking. It was fair sore getting it done, though. Your man has a wan working in the shop with him, I'd say she's Polish or something, and she'd put a horn on a dead man. Your man knows well no prick is going to chicken out of getting his tattoo while she's waving her tits into his face or walking past slowly, smiling, with her long legs and her beautiful arse.

Them apartments they give to slappers do be fair nice. They do kit them out and all for them, and not shite – proper stuff from Reids and all. The wan that had the child for me got a leather couch, two leather armchairs, a chandelier, a microwave, a fridge-freezer, the whole lot. I seen it all in through the door that time. I should of bursted in through the door and slapped the head off her and had a proper go at playing around with the young fella, but she told me fuck off, the welfare pricks were all over them like flies on shite that time, and I said ah come on, the *cops* are all over *me* and she roared WHAT! THE COPS? JESUS! FUCK OOOOOFFFFF! And the door of that rapid apartment nearly split in two she slammed it so hard in my face. Shite, I thought, I shouldn't of told her about the cops and stuff until after I'd the hole rode off her. Women do be less uptight after a ride. Especially off me – I'm fair good at it.

Like, they're all going mad off their heads around here, all the boggers, acting like the world is ending just because your man Bobby Mahon smashed his auld fella's head in. Their faces are all red and worried-looking. Your man that's dead was on the way out anyway. I often seen him out at his door, coughing his lungs up when I'd be passing down with the dogs. He was a freaky-looking bollocks. He'd never salute, only pull on his fag if he wasn't coughing and stare at me and I'd stare back and I'd have something smart all ready to shout over at him and then some feeling would come over me and tell me not to bother my hole and he'd hawk and spit and so I wouldn't. You have to trust your instincts when you're a dopey fuck like me. A sort of a cold wave came off that auld fella. He looked dark, even last week, when the evenings were shiny bright. No wonder your man Bobby killed the fucker. I'd say he did his head in.

YOUR MAN BOBBY is fair sound all the same. He tried to give me a job one time all right, but I'm not holding that against him. I think he thought he was doing me a favour. My auld fella brung me out to your man Bobby's house and all, the night before I was meant to start work on some mad lunatic building site or something. I'd look fuckin pretty on a building site, wouldn't I? State of me. But them FÁS cunts were making me seeing as I done a construction skills course and a Safe Pass yoke and the whole lot. I only done them to keep them happy at the hatch, I thought that was understood. I told your man Bobby, Jaysus sorry mate, I suffers awful from my back, and my head is all over the place, and he only laughed and said fair enough and thanked me and all for letting him know. Then he looked over at my auld fella's shiteheap of a Corolla and said Christ lads, that front wheel is buckled to bits and I said I know bud, it's like getting a spin in the Flintstones' car, ha ha ha, and fuck me if he didn't tell me hang on there a minute and went over to his big shed and rooted around and pulled out a fourteen-inch, four-stud wheel with a fair decent tyre on it and all and jacked my auld lad's car up and put it on and my auld lad was a fucking embarrassment saying ah, you're a decent skin, you're a decent skin, I'll pay you for it and all when I'm flush, and your man Bobby knew for a fact that was bullshit but he didn't give a shit. Yerra, it was only lying around here, he said, I don't even know where it came out of.

That's the way he was. The auld fella's car went sweet as a nut with that new wheel. Your man Bobby done that turn for fellas that was as good as strangers to him and looked for nothing back and nearly made it sound like it was us doing *him* a favour. I felt like some cunt after it. I wasn't even sure why.

Hillary

YOU KNOW, I don't think Réaltín realizes the trouble she causes half the time. Every single person in work knows about her going off with George at the anniversary party, but still it's me that has to get the evil eye off all the old bitches all day every day. It's grand for Réaltín, off on her so-called special career break. That was a new one for Georgie Pervy, the chickenshit bastard. Jesus, how are all men the exact same? George leches all over everyone, well, all the young ones anyway, and no one gives it a second thought, but Réaltín has to take it to the next level and actually shag him. But Réaltín doesn't care; she just does anything she wants. I'm not saying I don't love her, I really do, she's *gorgeous*, and she's brilliant craic and everything, but – I'd never say this to anyone – she's going to have to cop herself on. She's going to have to decide what she's doing with her life and stop being such a disaster.

I think sometimes it's an affectation, all the angst and introspection and random lovesickness, but then I see her sometimes, when she thinks no one's looking, and she just looks so sad. But she does draw sadness on herself, in fairness. I mean she's all of a sudden madly in love with this new builder fella. I think Réaltín actually thinks he's going to leave his wife and marry her or something. As far as I can make out he's not even made a ghost of a move on her, but she seems convinced he's besotted with her or something and it's only a matter of time before he drops his hammer and asks if she wants to see his other tool. She went off and bought about forty new outfits to wear for when he calls to her. And she's meant to be broke. She makes up reasons to get him to call. He charges her as well – nothing near what the cowboys in the city charge – but she couldn't have money to be throwing around on trying to seduce married builders. She got a hammer of her own (she probably stole it from his toolbox, in fairness) and banged a load of plaster off her bedroom wall and got him to fix it; she broke a cupboard door in her kitchen and let on Dylan did it; she broke tiles on the en-suite bathroom floor and got him to take them all up and do the whole thing again. And then while he's there she acts like she's a fucking little tramp, which she is, at times. She flits around him in skin-tight jeans or little minis, trying to make him make a move. And he hasn't, nowhere near, and probably never will now, because, you won't believe this: he's only after *killing* his own *father*.

First of all, she rang me about two weeks ago, crying her head off because old hatchet-faced Bridget, that married Réaltín's daddy (her and Réaltín are a lot more alike than Réaltín would want to hear; they'd both do anything to get their man), heard at some mad forty-five drive or bridge festival or somewhere that they were all talking about Réaltín in that crazy village where she insisted on buying that house, saying that her and this Bobby the Builder fella were having a proper affair, and he was moving in with her, and his wife was distraught and yadda, yadda, yadda. Réaltín's poor daddy got really upset; like, he must have known about the flirting, because he's always out there, making sure she doesn't get raped and pillaged by the mad villagers, cutting grass and trying to avoid Bridget the Midget probably, but he would have only rolled his eyes up to heaven and taken Dylan for a walk and left her at it, but those kinds of rumours going around would really make him feel terrible. He's lovely. He's *really* good-looking, too. He's one of those men who get even more hand-some as they get older, like Colin Firth or George Clooney. I had a little bit of a flirt with him, and I mean a demure, innocent flirt, at Réaltín's twenty-first and she went mental. She called me a bitch and cried and everything. What a fucking hypocrite! She nearly *raped* my father at my granny's funeral. His *mother*, like.

Anyway, as if that wasn't bad enough, that the whole crazy village thinks she's a brazen, home-wrecking hussy, now your man is after killing his own father. And you know there's a kind of inevitability about Réaltín being stuck smack bang in the middle of any drama in her vicinity. His own father, though, can you imagine it? He's been in Réaltín's house, at the top end of that spooky, empty, three-quarters built estate, and she's been bending over in front of him, wagging her little arse in his face, and all that time there was a murderer hiding inside in him. He just stove in the poor man's head, I heard. Sure, if he was capable of that he would have been capable of driving off with Réaltín and little gorgeous Dylan in his boot, tied up and suffocated to death. Oh Christ, it doesn't bear thinking about.

Some mad-looking cop, like your man out of *Killinaskully*, came up with a detective from town, asking her a load of ques-tions. The Bobby fella had been up in her house only that morning, imagine. They wanted to know what her relationship was with him, what they talked about when he was in her house, what his behaviour was like. They frightened the life out of poor little Dylan, who thought his mummy was being taken to jail, and they even suggested she leave him with her father and go to the garda station to talk about it. Fuckers. Luckily Réaltín was well aware of her rights, on account of George being the scumbags' solicitor of choice. Or he was, until the legal aid rates went down and George stopped being so available.

Oh lads, it's great craic now. Réaltín is acting like she's some kind of a victim of a miscarriage of justice. She's crying over your man non-stop, like. I had to remind her that she isn't his wife, she isn't his mistress, she isn't his friend – your relationship to him, I told her, is as follows: You are a fucking crazy single mother living in a freaky ghost estate who breaks things in her house and makes him fix them. That is not a relationship on the basis of which you have a right to be weeping at the foot of the gallows. He's not Braveheart, I told her, and you're not Braveheart's girlfriend. Sometimes you have to be firm with Réaltín. You have to tell her the truth. She gets lost in the mists of imaginary romance.

And there's more. As well as all of the above, it turns out your man Bobby the Murdering Builder knows Seanie well. Seanie is *from* that crazy village. She fucking knew that when she bought that house, but she never told me. It's mad, the things Réaltín keeps secret. Like, she'd tell me all about the colour of her poo, but she won't tell me something like that. And I'm serious about the poo. She went around the office one day in an unbelievable flap, convinced she had colon cancer or bowel cancer or something because her poo had turned green. It was the tannins from the bucket of red wine she'd glugged in my house the night before. But there was no telling her. Drama. Anything for drama.

She's a weirdo at times. Imagine how her poor daddy feels

now, having left her on her own in that house with a murderer! I wonder why he went and killed his father, anyway. A lot of those culchies are mad, though. They're so *repressed*, like. They all spend their whole lives going to Mass and playing GAA and eating farm animals and cabbage and not saying how they're feeling until it's too late and then BANG! They kill someone. Or themselves. They're just as mad as the city lunatics, except the city lunatics are honest about their scumbaggery. But anyway, Seanie the prickface is calling up now, roaring and shouting that she was riding his friend and crying like a baby and wanting to come in and staring down her top and licking his lips and sometimes, groping himself absent-mindedly. I only met him a few times, but I spotted that habit he had − it was dis*gust*ing − of talking to your tits and actually *licking his lips* at the same time. He's okay-looking, I suppose, in a rough sort of way, and he has a great body (that's how she met him, he was standing in a hole across the street from the office with no top on, just a skimpy luminous jacket thing over his jeans and a white helmet and Réaltín started acting like we were in a fucking Diet Coke ad or something), but he's an animal, really. Like, he's not civilized. He's not even *evolved*.

It's just like Réaltín to make everything about her, though. Someone gets murdered, and it's all about Réaltín. How *she* feels, how *she* is being victimized, how *she* can't go to the shop without people gawking at her with their big country mouths hanging open. That's Réaltín. She always asks how I am by rote; she never actually wants to know. If I started saying something like God, I'm exhausted actually, Mam is still really sick and I had to go home and make Dad's dinner, or God, I'm really pissed off actually, Darren never rang me since our row … her eyes would literally glaze over and she'd just say oh, aaaww, and tut-tut noncommittally a few times in mock sympathy, and get more and more impatient for the moment when she could start talking about herself. I mean, we're best friends since our first day in the School of Commerce, but it really feels sometimes as though I'm just a receptacle for Réaltín's thoughts and worries and complaints. I do love her, I really do, she has such a great heart, and she'd do *anything* for you, but she does think the whole universe revolves around her. Poor little Dylan, he's an absolute dote, but I wonder if she even knows he's there. Has she room enough in her head for a whole other human being, who's dependent on her? Sometimes I doubt it.

I don't know why I spend so much time talking about and thinking about Réaltín. She never bothers her arse to think about *me*, that's for sure. Like, I had to invite *myself* out to see her house. Then she tried to pick a day when her father wouldn't be there, in case I jumped on him or something, and then she rang to cancel because Mad Bobby the Murdering Builder was calling to suck sludge from her pipes or something, and I had the day booked off and everything, but she didn't give a shit. She suits herself, always. Mam was really sick last year, but I wasn't allowed to mention it, because her mother is *dead*, so that meant I couldn't be upset about my mother just being sick. When Darren broke it off with me, I couldn't get out of bed for about four days, but it was lousy of *me* to text *her* to tell George I wouldn't be in. I mean I was barely capable of speech, and absolutely incapable of coherency. Then she called up after about three days and all she could say was, ah Hillary, come on, he was a fucking *prick*, he didn't even have an *arse*, just a hole in his back! It was funny, and I did start to feel a bit better, but actual empathy is just impossible for Réaltín.

It was the exact same when we used to spend every single Saturday in town. Like, it was brilliant craic, and I loved being with her, but I used to have to spend literally hours sitting on chairs in dressing-room corridors, watching her parade up and down in outfit after outfit, reassuring her again and again that she didn't have a big fat arse. But if I ever tried anything on she'd be sighing and exasperated-looking and checking her watch (that I saved up to buy her as a present when Dylan was born) and saying ya Hillary, lovely, come on, I'm dying for a coffee and a bloody fag.

And when all that shit blew up a few years ago, when the recession had barely even started to kick in, with George telling her and me that since we were the last in and we were young and single, we'd have to take a massive pay cut because of the fall-off in conveyancing, I had to do all the arguing on our behalf. I was like, you know, Mister McSweeney, there's something in the equality legislation about discrimination on the grounds of age and marital status, and, ah, ammm ... And George, the sleazy fucking asshole, just sat there with his eyebrows arched in mock wonder and his hands shaped in a V, just under his narrow lips, and a little shitty smile, as much as to say go on, tell *me* the law, ha ha ha, and she just stood behind me, like she wasn't really party to any of this rebelliousness, but was just grudgingly supporting her errant friend out of loyalty, and she ended up *shagging* the old bollocks and getting a *special career break*, supposedly without pay, but I don't know. I still love her, though.

AREN'T YOU LUCKY to have a job? That's the stick that's being used to beat us all now. Like, you can't say one word about *anything* now, or you have that shit thrown at you. George sacked the cleaner. Then he started looking at *me*! The bastard. I was like, NO WAY, there's no *way* I'm hoovering *here* as well as at home in my parents' house because Mam is still sick with her mystery illness that not one doctor can diagnose in the whole country. And what about the goddamn toilets? Those horrible old biddies all shit like fat cows. There's no way in a *million* years I'm scrubbing their skidmarks. For anyone or anything. No job is worth it. So I had to kick and scream and cry until it was agreed that a rota would be drawn up among the secretaries for the cleaning, and everyone would have to do a day every three weeks. Then *I* had to scream that it was unfair; the apprentices and junior solicitors should have to as well. So George made the solicitors go on the cleaning rota to shut me up – he knows I know things about him, he's just not sure how much I know – but the sneaks always have an excuse: stuck in court all day, had to meet a client for early dinner, blah blah blah. So I'm stuck doing it most of the time anyway. For forty euros a week less than I used to get. But aren't I lucky to have a job? Ya, like, I'm *really* lucky.

Seanie

I DON'T KNOW in the hell where the name Seanie Shaper came
from. I remember lads starting to call me it in secondary all right,
but it didn't seem like a bad thing to be called so I let them off to
hell. Like, some lads got landed with awful doses of nicknames.
Your man of the Donnells from Gortnabracken got called Vomity
Donnell on account of he threw his guts up one time on the bus
going to a Harty Cup match; a lad from town got called Johnny
Incest because his parents were cousins; a fella that went with a
wan that was in First Year in the convent when we were doing the
Inter got called Kiddyfiddler forevermore. Another poor bollocks
was caught pulling himself in the toilet in the gym one lunchtime
and everyone called him Wankyballs from then on. There was a
lad called Fishfingers because he was forever taking wans from
the convent down the castle demesne at lunchtime and he'd give
the rest of the day smelling his fingers. There were about fifteen
lads from the real boondocks called Mongo. It was the townie

boys mostly who gave out the nicknames, and we all went along with them like goms. When all was said and done, Seanie Shaper didn't seem so bad a name to be called.

I was always a pure solid madman for women. I couldn't stop thinking about them from when I was a small boy. I used to chase girls around the estate out the Ashdown Road, trying to pull up their skirts. I used to try to bribe them for a look at their knickers. When I was thirteen, I got my first proper feel of a tit, off a wan from Dublin who was down visiting her cousins in the estate, down past our house. Your wan was sixteen. Her tit felt small and smooth, her nipple was hard. She wouldn't let me see it, only feel around under her T-shirt. I had a pain in my balls. She wanted to know did I want a go of her fanny and I only stood there looking at her, speechless. I panicked and ran. I wouldn't have known what to do with her fanny. Then I got sorry and ran back, but she was gone. I never saw her again; her cousins told me she was gone back to Dublin. It was three years before I got near a fanny again. I should have gone for glory that day behind the Protestant church.

I SUPPOSE that's where Seanie Shaper came from – I was forever fixing my hair and throwing auld smart shapes for fear there'd be girls along the road. I used to take a bit more care about myself than the other apes. I used to change my shirt *every* day, a thing unheard of in my circle. Some lads' shirts would be stiff with the dirt before it'd occur to them to look in the hot press for a fresh one. We used to sit on a wall across from the convent every day at lunchtime and the odd day a little ugly wan would come over to know would someone, usually me, go with her friend. I seldom refused. I even gave the little quare wans a go, in fairness. I went off with hunchbacks, lispers, smelly wans, lesbians, the whole lot.

I went with a wan one day who had a hearing aid and no front teeth. I got called a spastic-fucker for a few days after that but I didn't give one shit. God loves us all, in fairness. Them wans needed a bit of a good time too.

For a finish though, my lack of discernment began to damage my prospects. The desperate and demented began to rely on me for sexual initiation while the good-looking wans with the lovely blonde hair and long legs and flaking tits began to view me as a bottom-feeder, a bit of a dirty pervert, and, eventually, an untouchable. I started to hang around the Tech then and things improved again. I still believe I did good work at the convent with those unfortunate young ladies; I made them feel good about themselves and showed them how to give a handjob without rupturing a man's helmet. That's a valuable lifeskill. That'll have stood to them, I guarantee you.

WHEN I got older and started to do serious damage, I was always as careful as could be when it came to rubber johnnies. I always, always wore one, if not two. That Réaltín made an awful ape out of me. She told me she had an allergy to latex. She said she was on the pill. She scratched the back off of me. She went all night. She nearly killed me. I loved her. The first day I saw her, we were pulling a drain job inside in town, and she came out of an office across the way with her friend, that Hillary. She was shiny, dazzling, full of that scary confidence that some of them townie women have. Your wan Hillary looked like a browny-grey blob beside her. I was standing inside in a hole, gawking over at her like a redneck rapist when she actually *pointed* over at me. Then she turned to her friend and laughed, and the friend looked at me and smiled and looked away and I kind of knew then how girls must feel when we ogle them and pass remarks at them and laugh and whistle as they walk past us. She was in the Lobster Pot that night, talking to a right-looking wanker in a pair of slacks. I was full of bravery after a feed of pints and accidentally on purpose dropped a curried chip on his nice clean pants with the creases on them. Oh for *Gawd's* sake, he said, in his posh accent. What? I said. Are you throwing shapes there, boy? No, the poor prick said, and ran off like a little bitch. I took her back to the digs Pokey had sorted out for us and by the next morning, I was in love.

I got her up the duff and all, not long into the whole miserable thing. I think she wanted me to, like, she done it on purpose. She asked me a rake of questions about my family's medical history the night before the night she made me go bareback. Then she seemed to kind of get sick of me. She asked me to know if she moved out from town would I look after them and I said of course I will, and she bought one of Pokey's houses and all and I was kind of happy for a while, calling to see the small boy, but she seemed to get sick of looking at me or something and she started sniping and picking away at me and for a finish she fucked me off altogether and next thing I found out Bobby was tapping her, the two-faced prick. Bobby denied everything; he said he only went up to the estate to see was there any C2 boys above finishing off because we heard a rumour the NAMA crowd were after giving Pokey's da a rake of money back to do the rest of the houses and all, and she was there, and he hadn't a clue who she was and she asked him to know would he do a few jobs for her and it was only after about the third time he went over there that he realized who she was, and sure by then the whole village had it that he was riding her and I could believe what I wanted. And what could I say to that?

Bobby was the only one of us used to always go home after work, in fairness. He'd never stayed in the digs. He was pure solid wrapped in Triona, always. He'd never met Réaltín. I'd never said too much about her moving out here or anything. I don't know why I didn't. Maybe I didn't want to jinx it. My family was always into the whole mad Irish country thing of keeping secrets anyway. It's nearly like a kind of embarrassment, not wanting to say anything about yourself for fear you'll be judged or looked on as foolish.

I don't know in the name of God which way is up now. Bobby is after doing away with his auld fella, and Réaltín won't leave me inside the door, and her father, who's a quare sound auld skin, says I'm as well off leave her be for a while. Fuck that, though. He's my young fella too, like. I'm no good to him, though. What good am I?

I NEVER THOUGHT I'd ever be depressed, really. It's quare easy fall into that hole. You can kind of lose yourself very quick, when all about you changes and things you thought you always would have turn out to be things you never really had, and things you were sure you'd have in the future turn out to be on the far side of a big, dark mountain that you have no hope of ever climbing over. I was never idle a day since I done the Leaving. I got just enough for the apprenticeship and done my time as a steel fixer and Pokey gave us all jobs when his da handed over the whole works to him. We done everything: roads and houses and form-work and plant and drainage and the whole lot. Pokey tendered for everything. He took on a rake of Polish subbies and screwed the poor pricks and we all thought it was a laugh. That whole subbie thing was a right con job. Then he screwed the rest of us and we laughed on the other side of our faces. I still went around laughing and messing and joking and all, though. I'd never let nobody see how I was panicking.

Everyone thinks I'm gas, that I don't give a shit about anything. I never told anyone about the blackness I feel sometimes, weighing me down and making me think things I don't want to think. It was always there, but I never knew what it was until every prick started talking about depression and mental health and all that shite. I'm not a mentaller, like. I'm not. I just can't see for the blackness sometimes. It's always there, waiting for a chance to wrap itself around me. I often wonder why I was born at all, why my mother had to suffer to give me life, why my father bothered his bollocks with me, working his arse off to pay for things for me, everything I wanted, just about. I think of the ma and the da and how good they always were, and how they always encouraged me, even though it was pure obvious I was the waster in the family, and how they were so let down when I got Réaltín up the duff and they not even having met her and how they met her then and thought her shit was ice-cream, and they were nearly proud of me for a while, and they even thought I might marry her, and how they're solid heartbroken now over never seeing the child and all. It's all gone to shit. That's all my doing, how they're upset like that. Sometimes I feel short of breath and my heart pounds and I feel a whooshing in my ears and I double over and put my head in my hands and a few times lately my hands have been wet with tears when I've taken them away from my face. No fucker knows that, though, nor never will. I'll be grand in a while. I have no right to feel like this.

I think of the young fella, little Dylan, and how gorgeous he is, and how I always go about things the wrong way with Réaltín and accidentally look at her tits and she ends up pissed off with me and I always react like a right stones. I can't hold myself together at all, I gets pure wicked with her and tells her to fuck off and I can't tell her properly how I want things to be because I can't really think under pressure, when she's standing there, waiting for me to be a proper man. When I found out the other week that Bobby was above doing jobs for her I flipped the lid altogether; like, why couldn't she have asked *me* to do them jobs? But by then Bobby was after flipping his own lid and lamping his auld fella with a plank of wood across the poll. Instead of being reasonable and asking her what was the story, I charged up like a bull and started roaring out of me like a jackass and I frightened the young lad and her auld fella had to get thick with me and I took off over as far as Castlelough and sat on the low wall in front of the grass before the little pebble beach and looked out at the dark lake and thought about the bottomless hole that's meant to be out there in the middle of it.

A FEW years ago, a load of women from the same village up above in the back of beyond drove their cars to Castlelough and parked up and walked out into the lake. One at a time, over a few winter months. Them women all had husbands and children and all. I remember laughing about them women at the time, making stupid jokes about how all the boys up that side must be no use in bed and how I'd have cheered them up in no time and ha ha ha. Jesus. I laughed and I felt sick. I knew the feeling that drew them down from the mountain to the low, dark lake. There's a tug from that water. There's an end in it, under those little waves. Drowning is easy, I'd say. You only have to breathe in a lungful of water and you're gone, floating away to nothing. How come I can't be like everyone thinks I am? I'd love to really be Seanie Shaper. I'd love to not be here again, sitting looking at the water.

Kate

ONE AWFUL THING that happened since the recession started was Dell closing. Like, it nearly finished us. They were bloody *all* Dell. Dad said a few times I had all my eggs in the one basket, but I only told him to shut up and mind his own business, laughing at his little worried face. It does be all scrunched up when he's worried, the poor little pet. He was right to be worried, though – after Dell closed, I was paying more in wages than I was taking in for about three months – but I was never even close to giving in. You can't give your time whingeing and blaming, you have to just fight back. I made up a load of flyers on the PC and went to every single door in every single estate on this side of town, and covered a big part of the rest of town as well. I went over as far as Castletroy and Annacotty. Aren't they only out the motorway now? I didn't stop going for three weeks. My rates are the best anywhere. I promised to save people money. I prayed the HSE inspector didn't call for the three weeks, because my child-to-minder ratio was a bit off while I wasn't there. I made it back every day for the parents, though. I'm always there for hometime.

One good thing that happened since the recession started is people will work for less than the minimum wage. The minimum wage is a joke, like. Who has the right to tell me what to pay someone? Dad says there's no such thing as a free market while crazy laws tether employers to big huge salaries for their staff. He says Ireland is regulated into the ground. Like, the red tape! You wouldn't believe it. So I called all the girls into the kitchen one evening a few weeks ago and I told them straight out they'd all have to take a cut or I'd have to leave two of them go. Nuala, the little bitch, started straight away with the bullshit: You can't actually, you're right down to the lowest ratio as it is – we can't even take our *breaks*! That one. She spends most of her day on a break. I'd have given her the road last year but I know well she'd have me up in front of the tribunal. So I said, actually Nuala, I'd have to bring in my sister and my mother to help for a while, and you don't have to pay family members *anything*, so … And that shut her up.

THINGS ARE GOING great now again, thank God. This free childcare year is going to be the making of us. And better again, I got a Montessori teacher for feck-all – a fella walked in here with his CV and references who has a *degree* in childcare and a post-grad in Montessori teaching, with my ad in his hand. I know you'd never put a fella with that job, but he's not very masculine; there's a real soft look about him, and he has a lovely, gentle voice and nice blue eyes. Trevor, his name is. Imagine, I hadn't even to pay to put an ad in the *Limerick Leader*. I decided to give my window-ad a week and it paid off. Once I have his references checked, I'll let him start. He whispered to me that he wouldn't expect minimum wage, he'd do anything to be working, he'd take seven euro an hour, cash. I could gross up his wages to look right. He knew the lingo and all. Jesus, he's a godsend. To top it off, the Trevor fella arrived only two days after a girl called Réaltín called in with a lovely quiet child called Dylan. She's working in a solicitor's office inside in Henry Street. It's a big firm, too, and she said there's a couple more from there out on maternity leave. Having their *firsts*. She'll recommend me, surely. The way things are going I'll have to start refusing people again shortly.

Denis thinks I'm mad for taking on a *fella* as a Montessori teacher. But then he realized he used to know your man's father years ago; he was a dentist or something like that, near where Denis grew up, but they were real bigshots anyway, with a big high wall around their house. I'd say your man just wanted a job where he wouldn't have to be near manly men, spitting and farting and talking about their balls and making each other feel like shit about themselves. Why do fellas do that? They're always slagging each other and calling each other queer and trying to outdo each other like fools. Men working together shouldn't be allowed. Anyway, it's none of my business, I don't care what happens, I have my lovely Montessori teacher and I can take on kids for the free pre-school year and everything is rosy in the garden.

Sometimes I think Denis is a bit raging that my crèche took off like this. Isn't that awful? Like, wouldn't you think he'd be delighted? That's men, though; they can't bear to be second to a woman in *any* way. The time of Dell closing, Denis had nothing going on at *all*, there wasn't an electrical job or a carpentry job to be got anywhere, but we lived off the profits I had built up in the crèche account, and it nearly killed him. I felt sorry for him at the start, I suppose it was weird for him, but for a finish I just wanted to slap him and tell him to take the puss off him and just get on with it. He just has to do the small jobs again that he wouldn't have dreamt of doing five years ago. Hard luck, like. Build a bridge and get over it. God, Denis hates that phrase. He's some worker, though, I have to give him that. He just pretends there's no crèche now, we can't really talk about it. He doesn't mind the money shoring us up, though. God, like, I have to *pick* my *steps* around him these days. Why has he to be so sensitive? We haven't even had sex in about four months. He better not get any ideas about having a look around for himself. I'll cut it off of him. I'll cut it. Clean. Off.

The only thing pissing me off now is that little Nuala bitch. Like, if you saw her, the way she stomps around, acting like she owns the place. I caught her rotten the other week, hissing into a child's face. Just eat it, just eat it, just *eat* it, she was saying in a vicious little whisper, with a spoon of food pushed up against the kid's closed mouth. Jesus, she has a poisonous little temper on her. I pulled her on it and she was as bold as brass about it. What, she said, what am I meant to do? She wouldn't bloody eat her bloody lunch. Are we meant to let them get malnourished? I told her to never do it again and I was making a note of it and she wanted to know where was the note going to be kept, could she have a copy of the note, what was it going to say, who else was going to see it … For a finish I had to say, look, there'll be no note this time, but don't dream of being nasty to a child like that again. So she bested me. Jesus, she makes my blood boil. She had some comment up on her Facebook page one Sunday night a few months ago about going to work the next day, and my friend Liz saw it, something like OMG, sooo hung over, have to go wiping shitty arses all day tomorrow, and she must have gotten nervous because Liz says she took it down again straight away. I've been checking all their

Facebooks regularly ever since. They all know well, but they can't very well start blocking me now. Little witches.

WHEN DENIS was really quiet he still went off in his van every day. I didn't ask him where he was going. He was checking things out, he said. One day I asked him to put in some extra sockets in the kitchen and the nursery and he huffed and puffed and ummed and aahed about it. Can you imagine that? Oh, I said, Jesus, sorry, I thought you'd be delighted with the work! I was bitchy, I admit. Denis can be wicked when he wants. His father was a horrible bollocks; I'd say he gave Denis an awful time growing up. But wait till I tell you, that little bitch flounced in for her break and smoked a fag right outside the patio door, right beside where Denis was putting in a socket and I swear to God I saw the dirty prick looking up along her legs with his tongue hanging out like a dog on heat. And she wearing a little denim mini, which I specifically told her not to wear in work. Oh, it's so *hot*, she goes. Can I not just wear it *this* week? I also specifically told her not to be smoking fags on her break – one or two of the posh mummies have noses for smoke like bloodhounds. But she reckons she has some kind of right to smoke fags as well as everything else. I'll tell you what she has no right to do, though: wag her little arse in my husband's face!

You know the way when you start going with someone first, and you don't really mind if there's a bit of a smell off them sometimes? Like, I used to think Den's BO was sexy, because it meant he'd been doing physical work and was strong and manly. There's something about that, like, it's scientifically proven that women are attracted to men's body odours when they're in the first flushes of fancying a fella. But I'll tell you one thing – it soon wears off. Sweat is fine when it's fresh, on lovely hard muscle, but when it's dripping off a big flabby man-boob or dried into a filthy T-shirt it's a different thing altogether. When BO is just there because someone would rather sit on their arse watching soccer matches than have a two-minute shower, it's just repulsive. Although I suppose it was a bit lousy how I reacted the last time Denis tried it on with me. *Get your big sweaty arse away from me.* That *was* a bit harsh, thinking about it. He looked really hurt. He went off downstairs and put on the telly and watched his *Sopranos* DVDs for hours. I wonder if he cried? I think he thinks he's a bit like Tony Soprano.

I HAD a dream one night last week. Denis took Nuala for a spin in his van. I saw him stopping at the end of the cul-de-sac for her. I followed them down the road. I caught up with them in the car park outside the church. I crept up to the window of the van and looked in and they were in the back. She was straddling him with her little denim mini bunched up around her middle. The van doors were locked. I was shouting and screaming and slapping my open hands against the glass. It was like I wasn't there; they just stayed doing it. I could see right up Denis's hairy nose. He was lying on his back. He raised his head and looked straight at me and smiled. She turned around and smiled as well. Her teeth were small and sharp. The door suddenly gave way and I realized I had a hose in my hand. The hose streamed fire. I pointed it at them and they caught fire. I pushed the door closed and listened to them burning and screaming. When I woke up and realized I was dreaming I didn't feel that sick relief that usually accompanies waking from a horrible dream. I actually felt a bit disappointed. Jesus. What kind of a weird bitch am I?

Lloyd

I KIND OF THOUGHT actually that Trevor was gone completely
mental when he called up here a few weeks ago. Like, why would
he not text or email or Facebook? What's with all the reality, I
thought. Does he not know he's a million times cooler in virtual
form? God, he's misshapen. He wanted me to help him to *kidnap*
a *kid*. I thought he was pitching something to me, some concept
or something, some angle to keep the Dryffids guessing in
Warlock Universe – like the thing he thought of last year where
we hacked into their harems and stole all their girls (and boys in
Ming's case) and totally screwed up the spec of all their sex slaves
and made them into fat animal-headed creatures and wiped
out millions of their cred points. But he wanted me to actually
swipe a *living* child with him: he was going deep undercover as a
goddamn *Montessori teacher* in some nursery or something and
all I was meant to have to do was drive up, he'd hand over the kid
and I'd keep him for like, a night or some shit.

Mom was here like three weeks ago. I let her in this time. She saw my bong. I watched her for ages while she glanced at it, again and again. I knew she knew what it was. She was alive in the sixties, for fuck's sake. I hadn't left it out on purpose, but this apartment is so goddamn small that shit just piles up everywhere and you lose your ergonomic perspective. The bong was torturing her. I saw beads of sweat lining themselves up along the skin between her nose and her upper lip. What's that part of the body called? I can never remember. I started to really enjoy myself as her initial discomfort turned to pain and the pain wrote its signature across her stupid face. And I wondered what part of her was in me. Then I remembered. Every part. As she left she said please, Lloyd, please … and I said what, Mom? Please what? And I raised my eyebrows and half-smiled in a mock pleasantness that I know for a fact creeps her right out. Creeps *me* right out.

Just take care. I … I …

And she turned and scurried away, like a little white mouse, down the communal stairs and back to her terrified, dipsomaniac life.

MY DAD fucked off when I was a kid. I think he just couldn't stand to look at her any more. I remember the last time I ever saw him. He looked different, wearing a T-shirt and jeans and a jacket with the collar turned up. I remember thinking he looked really cool. He kissed me on the top of my head and said love you, kiddo. I didn't say anything back, just stood looking at him from the hallway, wondering why my mother was taking giant breaths and covering her face with one hand while pulling at my dad's arm with the other. Mom told me some bullshit story about how he had to go and do important work for the government to fix the hole in the ozone layer. I made myself believe that for years, until I overheard her on the phone to one of her mental-case friends, talking about him. He'd had another kid with another woman. A boy. I started to grind my teeth that night, and didn't stop for years, till finally I ground through to a nerve and the pain made me pass out.

I know now that all that shit was a series of tests I'd set myself. I think I failed some of them, that's why I'm still groping around in the dark.

I DREAMT I killed the kid. That kind of fucked things up, I can tell you. And not in the way you might think. I didn't mean it; I only wanted to see how far I'd go before I made myself sick and stopped. Then I woke up and the kid was standing up looking at me over the edge of the travel cot with his big scared eyes and I shouted *thank fuck* and frightened the crap out of him, literally. But being a solipsist, I know the danger of crossing boundaries in the dream dimension. It's a dream precedent; I know now it's an actual possibility. It's something my inner warrior wants to do and is not able to, being bound by the strictures of this false human reality. I still won't allow myself to be fully immersed in the truth: I am alone in the universe; the universe is created by me and for me and nothing exists outside of my consciousness. I have to explore the edges of myself. I have to learn more before I can break through the barrier. I have to not care about the feelings I ascribe to my creations. Why did I do this to myself, cripple myself with conscience? It must have some meaning, the fact that I *worry* about doing certain things, when I know that nothing has any consequence outside of me. It's another test I've set myself, obviously. But I don't know how to pass it – am I overcoming an obstacle by giving in to my urges to destroy, or by resisting them? What do I want from myself? Why am I so unknowable?

Having killed the kid in my dream bugs me, no matter what way I think about it. Now I don't know what to do. Opacity has trumped clarity again. These tests, these tests. Trevor has some meaning – he must be like a behaviour modifier or something. Obviously he's an integral part of me. He's an impulse, an instinct, a fight or flight mechanism. Him giving me this kid is me showing myself something. Maybe I should just ask straight out. I've always tried to stay icy cool around Trevor, though. I don't think he knows he doesn't really exist as an entity independent of me. Actually I'm sure of it. I need him to feel inferior to and fearful of me. I think that's how I'm supposed to make all my creations feel. It's easier with Mom. But then I've been working on her for longer. Solipsism isn't as easy as it might seem. It's difficult living in a universe with a population of one. But you already know this, being me.

I remember when I told Trevor I'd decided to be a solipsist. He laughed like a fat, retarded duck. He *honked* at me. Wow, he said, that's like a *really* good excuse to give yourself for not having a *job*. I disgusted myself by suddenly dropping my cloak of aloof superiority and becoming defensive. I can't help the *economy*, I said, in a pathetic, loser voice. *Pardon*, the bastard said, with glee in his eyes, *you* can't help the *economy*? But didn't you *create* the fucking economy, being a solipsist? And then he started to do his honking laugh again and I slapped him in his fat face. The tears that sprang immediately to his eyes fascinated me. I hurt him; I hurt myself. I felt my cheek sting later. This battle I'm having with Trevor is obviously some inner conflict, some breaking-down-building-up process of growing and strengthening, like a muscle being worked out. It has to be damaged to develop.

So, now I have this kid, who is wrecking my gaff. I've put myself in this position, that's obvious; I just have to figure out why. The kid is kind of cute. Dylan is his name. He keeps saying *Mama* and *Gaga* and crying and pointing, and the only thing that shuts him up is *showing* him things. Like, I have to pick him up and point at stuff and say look, Dylan, look at the stereo, look, Dylan, look at the cooker, look, Dylan, look at the fucking sofa. The kid loves looking at shit. I'm getting a bit pissed over this whole situation. Like, I could go down for this. I'd be in the news and everything. Sometimes I forget the solipsism thing and start believing myself to be vulnerable to outside forces. They're really *inside* forces; the things I'm afraid of are the weak parts of myself that I have to deal with. When I feel no fear, I'll have completed my journey. Then I'll become the being I was meant to be. I'm not sure what my true form is. I won't discover that until I've slain every demon.

Rory

THIS SUMMER was shaping up great and all. We had the World
Cup to look forward to – it's nearly easier to watch when we're
not in it – the weather was looking half-decent there around May
and late June, and Bobby was making shapes towards going out
on his own doing insulation and all that environmental shite that
everyone says is going to be the saving of us all. He rang me to
come up and all one evening and I gave a hand stacking blocks
of an ash tree he'd cut the evening before and he told me all
about it while we worked. I like that way of talking, so you haven't
to be nodding and agreeing and trying to hold a person's eye.
It gives you room to stop and think; the work fills the silence
between words. I went home delighted off my head. I even told
the mother and father about it. The mother got all dramatic like
she always does and started saying how she'd say a novena for the
plans and thank God for Bobby Mahon and the father agreed
away and he said begod tis the likes of Bobby will put paid to this

auld downturn and isn't he a solid sight to God altogether and if anyone could get something like that off the ground and running it was Bobby and stick with Bobby and by the end of the night I nearly hated Bobby and wondered why in the name of all that's holy I'd opened my big fat mouth about it at all. Still though, at least they were happy for a while.

Then Bobby went pure solid apeshit. That whole thing about him doing the dirt on Triona with Seanie's wan was all bullshit, but that was the start of all the madness. I reckon it was that crazy-looking auld bint that lives in the only other house in that estate that's lived in that started all that auld talk. She was forever eyeballing him going in and out doing them jobs for Seanie's wan. We didn't even know she was Seanie's wan till it was too late. The weird bollocks never told us nothing about her. He can be an awful oddball sometimes. But Bobby, though, if Angelina Jolie gave him the come-on he'd leave her hanging. He's like a fucking priest, so he is. Well, a priest that's married to a flaker. Then he upped and murdered his auld fella. I didn't know should I go up near him after he got out on bail. I never rang him yet or anything. What would I say? Howya Bobby, sorry you killed your auld fella? Maybe he didn't, in fairness. Jim Gildea came on him below with a length of timber in his hand though by all accounts, and the auld boy stone dead with his head smashed in. Bobby rang Jim and all to come down. Like he *wanted* to go down or something. He was a bad yoke, Bobby's da, a real twisted old fucker. Bobby must have finally had enough of his shit.

Whatever about that, I'm left high and dry now, without a hope of getting anything local, so my London plans are kind of back on and the mother and father are going around with two pusses on them like I was after telling them I have brain cancer or something. Every bollocks is going around cribbing about the country being fucked. It'd wear you out, so it would. The country's fucked, the country's fucked, the country's fucked; the same bollockses that were going around cribbing that the whole country was gone mad for money a few years ago. They do be below in the shop, standing in miserable little circles, comparing hardships. I'd love to tell them all they're a pack of miserable wankers only they're the same pricks I'll be looking for a job off of if things pick up or London doesn't work out, which it's looking like it won't, in fairness, on account of the auld fella going around like he's going having a stroke over it, saying them Olympics contracts is all stitched up, there'll be no Irish boys taken on off the boat no more, and the mother crying onto her rosary beads while she says novena after novena. Jaysus. How could I leave them like that?

I WISH I had an imagination, and more balls. I've thought about this – I think a lot more these days than I used to – and I reckon some are born to follow others. Like, Bobby is well able to think out all that stuff about going out on his own with the insulation thing and go off and talk to fellas about it and give in business plans to the enterprise crowd and look for money off of the Credit Union and all. I could do all them things too, only I haven't that thing that he has in him that makes all that stuff easy and makes people *believe* he can do it. It's a mix of imagination, balls, confidence and something else that I can't put words on. Something that makes you know he was born to give orders, not take them. It never looked right to see Pokey sitting on the chair in between the window and the desk and Bobby looking across at him with his back to the door. Pokey always made sure the chair facing the desk was smaller than his as well. He done his best to try and shrink Bobby and show who was boss. We all knew he was afraid of his shite of Bobby. Pokey was only boss because of his auld fella handing him over the whole works. It's Pokey should've had the bad auld yoke of a father and Bobby that was born with the silver spoon. Or would Bobby have turned out to be a sneaky little prick like Pokey then? God only knows how it works.

Sometimes thinking about things can balls you right up, though. I was inside in town the other day, looking at a poster for a gig in the Warehouse. A little flaker came up beside me and asked to know was I going. She had a tidy little pair of tits on her and short black hair and too much make-up on her eyes but I kind of like that, and I knew straight away without checking that she'd have a lovely arse and I managed to talk back to her no problem, probably because I hadn't been thinking about what I was going to say for five hours before I said it. I had a Pixies T-shirt on me and she told me she loved them and I looked a bit like Black Francis. What, I asked her, because I'm fat? And she went pure red and said no, no, Jesus, I meant your *hair* and stuff, oh God ... And I felt like a prick for embarrassing her like that and I said I was only messing and asked her did she see them in '04 and she said she was in the Phoenix Park *and* the Point and I said *I* was too and it turns out we were right near each other both times and after about three minutes I was starting to panic that this was going to be the highest point of my whole life, this random conversation with an accidental pretty girl on a dirty street while I waited to sign on. Here, she said, I have to go, I have an interview for a shitty job, call me out your number. And she sent me a text right there and then: *Holly* is all it said. So I know her name and I have her number and she likes the Pixies and before she walked off she said text me if you're at it and I said, like a dopey bollocks, at *what*? And she laughed and said the *gig* you fool and walked off laughing softly and I was right, she *had* a lovely arse.

The worst thing is I know I won't go in to that gig. I started thinking straight away about it. None of the lads will come with me and I won't go on my own. Isn't that unreal? And if I did manage to get brave enough to go in on my own, I probably wouldn't text her in case she was with a big load of her cool friends and they'd look at me like I was after crawling out of a dog's hole and they'd be in a big round of vodkas and Red Bulls and I'd have to go in on the round and I wouldn't have the price of it and I'd ask them all what were they having anyway like a big hard man and instead of going to the bar I'd sneak away out the door and run off home and later on she'd text me just a question mark and I'd probably throw my phone into the river out of pure solid embarrassment and shame at my own fear and uselessness.

FATHER COTTER used to say to us in school that a Christian, when faced with a moral dilemma, should ask himself only one question: What would Jesus have done? I've always stuck by that, except when I was young I substituted my auld fella for Jesus and when I got older, Bobby Mahon got the spot. How would I know what Jesus would have done? That fella was a mass of contradictions as far as I can see. One minute he says to turn the other cheek, the next minute he's having a big strop and kicking over lads' market stalls. He says blessed are the meek and he goes around shouting and roaring the odds to everyone. He rises from the dead and then shags off a few weeks later and leaves his buddies in the shit. If you look at it that way, Pokey starts to sound as Christlike as Bobby.

I could ask the auld fella for about seventy euro to go in to that gig and give him it back when my dole comes through. Pokey screwed us with the stamps so we have to wait for jobseekers or something. The father would give me it no problem, but then would he think to himself, haven't I a fine fella for a son, twenty-seven years old and tapping me for money to go to dances? Maybe he wouldn't think that, but even the thought that he might think it is enough to make me know I won't ask him. I could just text your wan Holly and say something funny, or just ask her how did she get on in her interview for the shitty job or send her a joke or something and if she texts back to know am I going in on Thursday I could have a good lie ready and that way there'd still be a chance with her but I wouldn't have the whole gig thing to worry about. But the gig is the big opportunity. I could easily get a chance to stick a head on her at the gig. I know she likes me; I'm not stupid. Flakers like her make it obvious, in a nice way, with laughs and eyes and questions put in a certain way. It's there for me, and I won't take it. I'll stay at home and watch *Coronation Street* with the parents, thinking about how thinking about things can stop you living your life. Thinking about Holly with some other prick that likes the Pixies, wiping the eye of a fella he never met.

I'll be in town again next week. I'll stand looking at the same poster, for a gig that will be over, wondering about the odds of her appearing again. I'll wear my Pearl Jam T-shirt this time. She was probably at that gig, too. I'll stand there until I start feeling like a dick, then I'll get the bus back to the village and look at her number in my phone while the summer rain runs down the window and my cowardly heart settles back into the slow rhythm of time being wasted. Then I'll delete her number.

Millicent

DADDY DONE a rudey this morning at breakfast and Mammy went mad. She called him a smelly bastard and told him farting was all he was good for. I felt sad for Daddy then because he looked sad on his face and he went all red and he said sorry love to Mammy and she started putting her arm over her nose and banging stuff on the table with her other hand and acting like she hated Daddy. Right after he done the rudey he smiled over at me like he always does and Mammy said don't be trying to bring *her* down to *your* level, you're a pure solid *show* opposite the child, you're such a bad *example*. I don't know what Mammy means half the time. Mammy told Daddy *I* was a better earner than *him* because I bring in a hundred and fifty euros a month and he brings in sweet fuck all. I heard her saying this before too. The child brings in more than you Hughie; the *child* brings in more than you. Mammy used to be always giving out stink to Daddy for accidentally saying that word in front of me but now she says it the whole time herself. It's a funny word. Fuck fuck fuck. I say it in my room but not so's Mammy can hear me. I test it out to see how does it sound coming out of my mouth. Daddy called Mammy a really bad word one night but I can't remember it but I know it must be real bad because he told her sorry straight away after he said it and Mammy was crying instead of shouting. Daddy doesn't have any work and he isn't allowed to get the dole because he was the boss of himself. Daddy says loads of words about the people who give out the dole. Real bad words. Daddy says he built the country with his own bare hands while they were inside drinking tea. Mammy tells him ah shut up.

MAMMY WORKS in Tescos. She told Daddy she has to work her fingers to the bone. I cried when I heard Mammy saying that. I thought all the skin was going to come off her fingers. I thought her fingers would fall off. Like that man in the village whose leg fell off and now he has a leg made out of metal and he does be drunk and falls on the footpath and people have to pick him up and Daddy tells me don't be looking at him, and one time we were coming home from Mass and we seen him falling over and Mammy said oh Hughie pull over and give him a hand and Daddy said he would in his bollocks, that fella was only a knacker and he could stay inside in the gutter. Mammy gave out the whole way home telling Daddy how it was awful to be coming from Mass and he wouldn't give a proper Christian example to the child and how would he like if it was *him* who was lying in the street and people driving past him and walking out over him. Daddy said nothing back to her only got redder and redder and then when we were eating our dinner later on I saw a big long snot from my nose falling into my gravy like a little waterfall and then I knew I was crying and I didn't really know why. I get really sad and I start crying before I know I'm going to. Then Mammy and Daddy always stop fighting and stop not talking and do start hugging me and saying sorry, sorry darling, sorry little love, oh it's not *your* fault, sorry, sorry, sorry. I don't know what they do be on about half the time.

Daddy collects Mammy and Assumpta Gill from Tescos. All the other fellas driving their cars are only pricks. I shout PRICKS and Daddy does laugh and says not to be saying bold words. Then I do shout it again and he laughs again and pretends to be cross. YOU'RE ONLY A PRICK AND A BOLLOCKS I do shout out the window like Daddy does and he says MILLICENT! And I know well he does be only letting on to be cross with me. He always smiles back at me straight away after. Daddy in the mirror is always smiling when Mammy isn't with us. Daddy in the mirror is always sad when Mammy is with us. Daddy in the mirror never sings on the way home from Tescos, only on the way in. Assumpta Gill smells like fags. She does be telling Mammy about all them little bitches in work and how they're all real sly. They do be forever getting Assumpta into trouble, licking on her. Mammy agrees away with her. Then when she's gone, Mammy tells Daddy she's an awful silly cow. I never say any bad words in front Mammy and Assumpta Gill because I don't want to get Daddy in trouble.

I'LL BE GOING back to school soon at the end of this summer and then Daddy won't be minding me any more and he does be saying what'll he do without his baby girl in the mornings, he'll have to go way and get a real job besides sitting down on the couch with me looking at Iggle Piggle and Peppa Pig and I feel real sad when he says that because I don't want to go to school and leave my daddy all sad without me and it'll be no good watching Peppa Pig without me. How's it daddies can't come to school anyway? Maybe they'll have to now if everyone is still going around scared of the Children Snatcher Monster. A child got kidnapped in the city and the child was belonging to a lady that lives up the road from our house and the child was took away by a fella in a car from the house where he was getting minded near the big huge shopping centre inside in town. Mammy had her hand over her mouth when her friend came in to tell her about the lost baby and she kept saying oh sweet Jesus, oh sweet Jesus, oh sweet Jesus, and she started crying and then I started crying because I got an awful fright. Then Daddy came in and Mammy started giving out stink to Daddy saying you better not ever take your eyes off of her, do you hear me, don't ever take your eyes off of her, and Daddy just stood there saying of course I won't, and Mammy said sure I don't know what way you mind her when I do be at work, sure you're an awful eejit, you could let her run out onto the road or anything, and she kept giving out and giving out and I said Mammy, Daddy is brilliant at minding me, I wouldn't ever go out near the road, Daddy never takes his eyes off of me, and then the two of them had a fight over me trying to hug me at the same time and Mammy was trying to hug me and so was Daddy at the same time, and Mammy was pushing Daddy away until Daddy started *crying*, and I got an awful worser fright than when Mammy had started crying because daddies *never* cry and Mammy must of felt right sorry for giving out stink to Daddy because she went real quiet and rubbed his arm up and down and held his hand and Daddy was trying to hide his face with his other hand and they must of forgot about me then because they started hugging each other like mad and I didn't mind them having forgot about me for a while when I seen that.

Then later on I was sitting up on Daddy's lap and I was after finishing my secret bottle that I'm still allowed have before I go down to bed even though Mammy says I'm way too big now to be sucking bottles like a baby and Daddy was rubbing my hair and I could feel the warmness of his breath on the top of my head and he was whispering I love you baby girl, I love you baby girl, I love you baby girl, and he kept saying it over and over until I was nearly asleep and when he took me over for a kiss off Mammy before he took me down I seen her give *him* a kiss as well and I felt real happy. But now I'm not able to go asleep because I heard Assumpta Gill saying to Mammy imagine he's still out there, there's a monster out there who snatches children imagine, oh Lord save us and guard us, Assumpta Gill was saying, but I wasn't afraid of the Children Snatcher Monster when I heard Assumpta Gill saying it to Mammy earlier because Mammy and Daddy were there on either side of me and it was sunny outside and no monster would be able to steal a child on a sunny day in front of her mammy and daddy but now I'm in bed and Mammy and Daddy are off down the hall and through the kitchen and inside in the sitting room and the Children Snatcher Monster could easily be hiding outside in the hot press and my night light is no good at keeping away the dark because my room is full of dark over around the wardrobe and at the bottom of my bed and all. I don't want to be calling Mammy or Daddy though because they might have a fight again over me being scared and Mammy might blame Daddy for me being scared.

I'll hide in under the blanket. I won't move and if the Children Snatcher Monster comes into my room he'll think there's no one inside in the bed. I'm not going calling Mammy or Daddy. I'll roar and scream at the Children Snatcher Monster if he comes near me the way Daddy roars at the pricks and bollockses and stupid fuckers in the other cars and the way Mammy roars and shouts at Daddy over all the things Daddy done wrong to leave us without a bob to our name only what she gets from the poxy few hours that fat bitch allows her on the roster inside in Tescos. That roster does make Mammy awful cross. I wonder what sort of a yoke it is at all. Is a roster as bad as a dirty owl tramp? Mammy said one time that that's all Daddy's mammy is. Daddy's mammy is my other nana. I never seen her. I'll use the awful word Daddy said to Mammy, so I will, if that Children Snatcher Monster comes near me. I'll say my prayer over and over again. Saying your prayers is the same as talking to Holy God so it is. Oh Angel of God my guardian dear to whom God's love commits me here ever this night be at my side to light and guard to rule and guide. Amen.

Denis

YOU'D OFTEN SEE lads in films that are thrown in jail and afraid of their lives or being held prisoner and after getting the shite bate out of them, lying curled up with their knees up near their chins. The *foetal* position it's called, because that's the way a child lies in the womb. Small children do often lie that way in their cots to give themselves comfort. They're reminded of the warmth and safety of the time before life. Them lads that are thrown in jail in the films are looking for that comfort back. There's something in it; I know that. I've been lying that way for days now. Kate thinks I'm sick. She was in a right flap the first day because she never seen me sick before. I was never sick a day in my life. Now she's only barely tolerating me. She isn't far off of telling me cop the Jaysus on and go out and get things sorted out in the name of God before the sheriff comes and empties out the house. The crèche is closed since the child went missing. I haven't a snowball's chance in hell of a job. I'm owed a small fortune. The sky is falling down.

I drove around the country for weeks looking for Pokey Burke and Conleth Barry and four or five more bollockses that owe me money. I'm owed near a hundred grand. I had the taxman roaring in one ear and the lads roaring in the other ear, and plant strewn all over the country. I done four or five jobs there I was never paid a cent for. I done them on the strength of jobs done before where I was paid as I went along and there wasn't enough hours in the day to get the work done. It's always the subbies gets shafted for a finish. I have thousands of miles done looking for lads. I didn't even know as I was driving around like a blue-arsed fly what I'd say if I found any of them. We done the second fixing for a hotel for a fella from Limerick – kitchens, stairs, bedrooms, ballroom, boardrooms, the whole shebang. Then it all went wallop and he done away with himself. What was I meant to say to his widow? Go handy there on the big spread for the funeral, hey, I has to get paid yet?

Things was building up a long time inside in me. I nearly drove over a gimpy lad up above in Lackagh that wouldn't leave me in to a site to take plant back. There was no bollocks else up there; I could easily have drove out over him. I thought about it and all, gave it proper consideration. He'll never know how close he came to being shipped back out foreign, flat-packed. I nearly went in through a plate-glass door of an office of a fat arsehole in Galway that wouldn't come out and talk to me. I would've been happy with a promise, with a sorry, with a pay-you-next-Tuesday. I knew he was in there and he wouldn't come out. I was standing outside his door, roaring in, and the little blondie wan behind a desk inside wouldn't press the button to leave me in, she only sat there looking out at me with her mouth open. I had to take a hold of myself and close my eyes and make myself breathe slowly and deeply. I saw silvery stars, floating and popping in front of my eyes. I went back and sat in the van a while and smoked a fag and listened to my heart pounding in my ears. Palpitations, that's called, when you can feel your heart beat. Then I pulled the wipers off of his Mercedes and fucked off. Imagine that. I pulled the wipers off of his car, like a bold schoolboy.

I couldn't think as I drove the roads. I couldn't listen to the radio. Whingers on Joe Duffy moaning and groaning about their shitty little problems, little jumped-up know-it-alls rattling on and on and on about whose fault it all is. Fellas that never done a day's work in their lives, besides spouting shite about how everyone is wrong except them. They'd make you puke. How's it they all have squeaky voices? They have the whole country afraid of their own shadows. I killed a man. There's nothing as bad as a wanker who thinks his shit doesn't stink, with a poncey accent, talking about how things was done all wrong. FUCK OFF, FUCK OFF, FUCK OFF, I shouted at the radio as I drove. Shouting at the radio. Isn't that some waste of energy? I killed an old man. Kate wanted to know every evening how much did I get, did I send the invoices by registered post, did I call to the bank to know would they extend the overdraft, did I get back the plant? I sat there a few evenings picturing myself punching her into her mouth. I sat thinking about hitting my wife, and that was the only way I could *stop* myself from hitting her. She didn't know. She doesn't know me. Then I killed a man.

I knew Pokey Burke's foreman was still knocking about the sites. I knew he had stuff took out of some of the houses, and not just the ones Pokey done himself – he had stuff swiped out of our ones too. The subbie always gets shafted. I heard he was still over abroad in Coolcappa now and again and he and a foreign lad and a couple more was doing patch-up work on a few of the houses in that disaster area out along the Ashdown Road. I drove over in Kate's car one morning and I seen him coming out of a house up above near the top of the estate. Your wan whose house it was walked out along with him. She had a child in her arms. I drove off again, feeling like I shouldn't have been watching him, like he was a fella like me and I shouldn't be blaming him for the sins of another. Then I started thinking more about him and the thoughts kind of heated up and burnt the inside of my brain. He was always stuck to Pokey like shit to a blanket. Pokey always got his approval for the smallest plan – when to pour concrete into formwork, when to start foundations, when to eat his sandwich. Pokey hadn't a hand of his own.

One of the lads told me your man Bobby went down every single day to his home-house where his father still lived, away off down past the weir. I said I'd corner him on the road and ask him to know where was Pokey and what was happening with the sites and did he know anything about the finances. I thought I'd get it all out of him; he's a fella like me, we were forever smirking over at each other during them meetings Pokey used to love having. We were on the same level, I thought. I knew the father's house straight away; Andy said there was a couple of acres of briars and brambles alongside it and a slatted house with a hole in the roof. I drove the van a half a mile down the road and up a boreen and crossed back through fields to the stone wall across from the cottage. Andy told me your man Bobby often walked down for his visit. I said I'd wait and watch across for him. Then I thought about him knowing where Pokey was and protecting him to feather his own nest and I got vexed and impatient and went in along the yard. I had it in my mind to ask his father where was he, the way the auld fella would think there was people looking for him and he mightn't be thinking he had a grand boy for a son whose shit didn't stink. I wanted the father to know his son fraternized with rats. I wanted to frighten him. I wanted to frighten someone, *anyone*, so I wouldn't be the only one feeling this way.

There was a red metal heart, spinning in the breeze in the centre of the low front gate. The hinge was loose but rusty, it squeaked and creaked but still allowed that little heart to spin. It reminded me of my palpitations. I drew a kick at it as I passed in. I pushed the front door; it was solid and heavy. I pushed again and it opened. He was expecting his son. I didn't know until then that I had a length of timber in my hand, I swear on my life. He was standing inside in the dark kitchen, in that crooked-legged, bent-back way that some auld boys have of standing, like they don't know whether to take a step forward or fall down on their arse. He looked at the timber and then up at me, and he laughed. His laugh reminded me of my own father, the time I came home with my eyebrow split and my collarbone broke after we lost to Roscrea in the under-sixteen championship. My father looked at me that day and my face streaked with blood and muck and tears and he laughed that same shrill laugh and he told me I was nothing but a useless cunt.

Are you going robbing me? Bobby Mahon's father wanted to know. He was pure matter of fact about it. He asked the question the very same way you might ask a lad is he going making a mug of tea. You're a fine boy, he said. And he laughed again. His laugh made my eardrums vibrate, the way a child's cry would. Go on away, you prick, there's fuck all to rob here. Unless you like corn-flakes: I have rakes of them. Is that what you're at? Robbing corn-flakes off of old men? Then he smiled at me and his eyes shone and in a soft voice he said you're nothing but a useless cunt, and I nearly fell backwards, back out the kitchen door. Did he really say it, or did I imagine it? You're nothing but a useless cunt, he said. Or did he? I'll never know now. He started laughing again, and my eardrums vibrated again, and my eyes went a kind of blurry. I took two or three steps forward and I saw him bracing himself and he spat sideways and looked straight into my eyes just before I lamped him as hard as I could into the fucking bald old poll.

GOD HELP ME, I thought I was killing my own father, just for them two or three seconds, just for that time that'll be the rest of time for me, I swear to almighty God. I killed Bobby Mahon's father, a man I'd never before in my life laid eyes on and I'm lying here ever since, curled up like an unborn child, with my murdering hands between my knees and my guilty heart pounding, pounding, pounding in my ears.

Mags

I OFTEN WATCH Dad feeding those chickens. He has pure fools made out of them. They go crazy when they see him coming; they know well he'll have a fistful of caterpillars for them. They flap up and down and nearly fly over the wire. Dad stands with his back to the house, facing the chicken run, talking to them. I'd love to know what he says. I've often thought to try and sneak out along behind him and listen, but I know I'd only embarrass him. He'd turn around and catch me creeping along his carpet of grass and he'd jump and be embarrassed and I'd laugh like an idiot and he wouldn't know what to say to me and I'd ask was he having a nice chat with the chickens and he'd just mumble something back at me and we'd have to walk back into the house together and every step would be a torment to him. If I stand at the kitchen window and just look out at him, I can imagine that if I went out to him that he'd be delighted to see me and he'd put his arm around me and we'd look at the chickens and he'd tell me about how

Henrietta is a real old bossy-boots and how she bullies the rest of the fatsos around the place and how he spotted an old sneak of a fox the evening before, looking in over the stile behind the workshop. The way he talks to Eamonn and my niece and nephew.

A CHILD went missing a few days ago from a crèche inside in town. The little boy's mother is living out here, in one of the houses in Pokey's famous nearly empty estate. Mam says Dad is taking it awfully hard, as though he's responsible by proxy for the girl living out here and having her child in a crèche inside in town because she has to work so hard to pay her huge big mortgage. And what about Bobby Mahon, killing his father! Well, he's supposed to have, anyway. That girl whose child was taken from the crèche is a blow-in, Mam says. *Blow-in.* That phrase is used so derisively. As if to say it's a failing to not have been born and bred here, to have settled in a place outside of the place of your birth. Mam doesn't mean anything bad by it, though. It's hard to shake your prejudices, I know. The guards are all over the place; it's putting everyone on edge. Someone just pulled up outside that crèche and drove away with the little boy. There was a Montessori teacher with the children at the time, and four or five qualified childminders in a room next door. The Montessori teacher was taken in and questioned. He's at least guilty of criminal negligence. It doesn't seem natural for a young *man* to be a Montessori teacher. Jesus, imagine if Ger heard me saying that! Prejudice, how are you.

I OBSESS about the moment that I knew Dad was gone from me, where that delicate balance between love and shame tipped in favour of shame. I was working for a charity that sunk artesian wells in developing countries stricken by drought. We built the wells and instructed people in the construction process. I loved it. I still love it. I was home for a weekend and Mam had invited their best friends for dinner. I knew she wanted them to hear about my work; she was so proud of me. I'd graduated with a first and was working as an engineer *and* was helping people. And because I'd worked in Africa, it was almost as if I was *on the missions*. Mam never mentioned or seemed to notice the steady seeping away of my femininity. She always seemed interested in what I was saying. She smiled at me and nodded in agreement while I galloped around the kitchen on my hobby horses: Palestine, global warming, oil-motivated wars, child soldiers. She seemed to really like Ger; I presumed she knew; I was impressed by her forbearance, her acceptance. I kind of thought Dad was the same, just less obviously so.

Then, at the infamous dinner that weekend nearly three years ago, while I talked about the potential for wiping out cancer using viruses that can be modified to locate and destroy cancer cells, Dad started to tut-tut and roll his eyes up to heaven. I thought he was tutting about the pharmaceutical giants that I was blaming for curtailing research into virus-cures. I was mostly quoting Ger. Thank God she wasn't there. Man has such huge potential, I was saying. *Man* holds the key to the wiping out of disease, in his enquiring mind and insatiable appetite for knowledge, *man* has ...

And all of a sudden, in front of Doctor Roche and his big fat wife Kathleen, and Pat Hourigan and Dorothy with her shrieking tipsy laugh, and the Crawfords who Dad always did business with for years and years and Uncle Dicky and Auntie Pam and my halfwit cousin Richard, and Mam, and Eamonn, and Eamonn's lovely wife, and Pokey with his little sly smirks and constant aura of having been hard done by, in front of all of them, Dad looked straight at me, and put down his wine glass, and said, in a voice that I hardly recognized, louder than he'd ever used at the dinner table: *Man* is it? *Man* is great, is he? You're all about *man* all of a sudden, aren't you? I thought your crowd was always *down* on *man*.

Your crowd? He meant lesbians, I knew. I felt this strange fuzziness in my stomach, and a tightening in my throat, and my mouth became instantly dry. I said that I meant man as in *humanity*. My words sounded whining and tiny and pathetic in my ears, like little fists banging on a stout, bolted door. I felt dizzy, the sickening vertigo that a sudden shock can bring. I felt like running away and vomiting and curling into as small a ball as possible and crying for days. I felt a sudden longing for my childhood bed and my battered, one-eyed Teddy and for Daddy to come wordlessly in and kiss me on the forehead and brush my hair back with his rough, lovely hand. I knew then that he didn't accept me as I was, he wasn't the man I'd thought, he wasn't able to cast away the sting of stigma like an annoying thistle from his vegetable garden the way I'd imagined him doing. The other people at the table were all looking at their plates. Dorothy shrieked once and whimpered twice and slurped stupidly from her empty wine glass. Let me top you up, Dad said to her, in a normal, ordinary voice. The spell of mortification was broken. I ran from the room and nobody followed me, and I got my coat and drove away and didn't come back for nearly a year.

IT TOOK ME AGES to understand what happened on the Horrible Sunday. Ger's objectivity helped. She said parents have a vision for their children and their disappointment when that vision isn't realized can manifest itself in anger. And it can be far worse when a child *seems* to be fulfilling their hopes, and then all of a sudden, as they see it, they veer off course. Is discovering your sexuality really *veering off course*? It is when the parents' vision is centred on marriage and grandchildren and what they would see as convention and normality, Ger said. And *safety*. Leaving the herd isn't safe. You're the loose gazelle that the lion will chase. A child putting themselves in danger, physically or emotionally, can trigger a reaction in a parent that comes out as anger directed at the child, but is really their anguish and worry, verbalized in an inappropriate or awkward way. But the things Dad said, and the way he said them, were so scarily unlike him, so cutting, so cruel. That's just the way he was reared, Ger reckons. She says people's thoughts, when their upbringing is mired in dogma, aren't really their own. Their opinions are twisted, not reflective of what's in their souls; their words are delivered obliquely, like light being refracted through water – you can't see their real feelings, just as you can't see the true position of an immersed object.

So Dad is drowning in prejudice, basically. Ger laughed at that. She thinks it's hilarious that I always look for the bottom line, the succinct phrase to describe a situation. You should be a politician, she says, you love *sound bites*. I must get that from Dad, that impatience with the abstract, that inability to concentrate on something that bores me, the desire to have things clearly and neatly and *safely* defined and compartmentalized. An old lecturer once told me I tended towards being dangerously reductive. Dangerous! Ha. I feel anger at things that I see as wrong. Many hold opposing views to me. Is it so bad that Dad has a problem with same-sex relationships? I wonder if he'll be more or less accepting now that the law has changed and Ger and I could, if we wished, give ourselves the same standing in law as heterosexual couples. I suspect that our nascent legitimacy will only entrench him further. I don't care, though, if he can never feel the same pride in me that I know he used to. I just want him to remember how he loved me. I want him to know I'm still his little girl.

Jim

A MAD OLD BIDDY burst in here earlier on. How is it ye couldn't have kept that dirty animal locked up besides leaving him out to terrorize the women of Ireland? And how is it at all ye can't find that little boy that was took? A little boy from out around *here*, you know! He's out there somewhere now; probably being fiddled with and having his picture took by perverts, *if* he's even *alive*! And now that other filthy fucker is out around the place, and who's to say he isn't in ca*hoots* with whoever whipped that little young fella from under the noses of them townies inside? Look at the timing of it! Oh Lord. Oh Lord spare us.

And then she gave a couple of minutes crying and hegging and catching her breath. First I thought she was on about Bobby Mahon, and then I remembered all the mad hullabaloo on the news about that fella of the Murphys getting released. Nobody wanted him to be left out, I told her, but the law is the law. He has his time served. *Time*, she roared. TIME? What about all them missing girls? Who'll give *them* back their time? Yerra, there's no evidence to say he had anything to do with any of that, and anyway he'll be back down around Baltinglass or wherever he's from, I told her, a hundred miles or more from here.

There was no consoling her, though, and no moving her from the station door. She stood roaring in at me at full pelt for a solid half an hour. She saw a fella that was the spit of him thumbing a lift out on the Esker Line. He had the very same cap on him the hoor was wearing when he sauntered out of jail. She'd swear her oath twas him. Oh Lord save us and guard us isn't it a fright to God to say children can be stole and good men battered to death in their own kitchens and rapists freed in the same few days? And there's talk now of the pension being cut! Isn't it an offence to His eyes to have to watch while people is left without protection from penury or madmen? What's after happening to the country at all? Then she started on about how she was going taking all her tablets together and going off to bed and not waking up any more and I nearly told her go on so, you'd be as well off, you mad bitch. Thank God I caught myself in time. I blame them bigmouths on the radio and the television for a lot of this hysteria that's after overtaking people. They fatten on the fear of others, them bastards.

I HAVEN'T SLEPT in four days. I watch the shadows on the curtain cast by the light of the street lamp outside our house as the breeze strokes the branches of the elder. Sometimes the branches take the shape of a giant reaching claw. All I think about is that little boy, and where in the name of God he could be. I lie there under a sheet of sweat and wonder is there a sort of a balance, a symmetry that the universe must achieve, the way water must always find its level. I led my sister Bridie's little lad into mortal danger years ago; I let him be washed off of a rock and swept away. I took my eyes off him for a second and he was gone. I should have thrown myself in after him besides standing on a rock, roaring out at the wild ocean. I should have carried him into Heaven. God only knows the dark, cold place his little body lies.

God knows where this child is too, and I wish God would tell me. I wish I could sleep and dream of where he is and wake and go and lead him by his little hand back into his mother's arms.

I've been on the search party every day. The forensics lads put us into a line and tell us to link arms and take slow steps, looking down, looking left and right. Each person has his own arc, but they should overlap. We've covered every bit of ground in twenty square miles. But he was taken in a car. He could be anywhere. Now I'm told stay put in the village, the village needs an operational hub. A pure public relations stunt is all that is. Young Sean Shanahan is little Dylan's father. It was the end of the first day before anyone knew that. Everyone thought that girl was a blow-in, no one knew she had such a solid link to the place. Not that it'd make any odds or anything. Young Shanahan is tearing around the place like a madman. He roared in the window of the squad car at Philly that we were only a pack of wasters. Philly said the tears had tracks made down his face the very same as scars made by a knife. The child's mother was with him, pulling him back by the arm and telling him calm down. She's a tough yoke, that lady. Réaltín, her name is. That's a lovely name. I'd have given my daughter a name like that if we'd had one, if the universe hadn't to have its symmetry. Her father is a grand man as well, he's as pale as a ghost going around, but he's been going non-stop since the first hour. He's being pragmatic and realistic and hopeful, just the way you have to try and get people to be in these situations. That's what the Civil Defence boys say anyway. He was an accountant I think. He's not losing it the way young Shanahan is. Young Shanahan now would want to catch a hold of himself.

It doesn't seem right to even be in a bed these days, not to mind sleeping. Since midsummer things are gone pure haywire. I wouldn't have said Bobby Mahon killed his father any more than the man in the moon. But he rang me that day and asked me in a soft, flat voice to come down to the house and when I got there he was standing in the kitchen, looking down at his father in a puddle of blood with a piece of timber in his hand that was wet with red. When I asked him was it he did it, he told me he didn't know. He didn't *know*, you know. He didn't say another word, only sat inside in the interview room inside in Henry Street as pale as a ghost and as silent as the grave. And the whole place has it he was doing a line behind his wife's back with the mother of the girl whose child is gone missing. I said to Mary it's the very same as something you'd see happening in one of them programmes on the television. Mary says I'm raving through my arse saying young Mahon didn't do away with his father. I can see her point of view. But I know in my heart and soul he didn't do it. I wish I knew how I knew, and then I might be able to figure out what really happened. I wish Bobby would snap out of this waking coma he's after falling into and start talking properly. Josie Burke put up his bail. Josie might get sense out of him.

YOUNG TIMMY HANRAHAN walked in here not long after the mad roaring biddy. He looked at me out of his mouth for at least a half a minute while a tide of red rose in his face. He scratched himself a couple of times before he spoke. Finally, he said he heard a lad saying awful quare things on a mobile phone the day before at the very back of the search-party meeting where he thought he couldn't be heard and he was on about going to jail for twenty years and he asked the person on the other end to know had he been watching the fucking telly and did he realize how many was looking for clues about the child and what have you and isn't that fierce funny auld talk, Timmy wanted to know.

Timmy described the boy he'd heard talking on the phone and I felt a kind of a burning in the pit of my stomach. There's one twitchy-looking little fucker does be around every day, mooching around the edge of the tape and trying to talk to the forensics boys. He was in a few of the parties that went in around the forestry over around Pallas where a car was seen like the one described by the children that were looking out the window that day. I might be clutching at straws now, but I have another strong feeling, the very same as I have the feeling about Bobby Mahon not having killed his father. I have a feeling that that twitchy prick and the Montessori teacher are kind of, I don't know even how to put it – the *same*, sort of, like they're the same *type* of a fella, kind of brainy and a bit odd and *outside* of things, even when they're in the middle of goings on. Who ever heard of a young lad doing that job, anyway? Your lady that owns the crèche says she had him checked out and all before he started, but there's no record on the PULSE of any check being done. She's a quare hawk, that one; you wouldn't know what to make of her. She's finished in the childminding business anyway, that's for sure.

But that Montessori teacher is awful suspicious if you ask me. I can't understand why the crowd inside in Henry Street aren't making more of that. He says he let the young fella out the door two steps ahead of him and the car was waiting near the door and the lad climbed into the back seat and even as the car drove off his only thought was that it was very rude of Dylan's dad to just take him without saying anything, then in the next second he thought maybe it was a snatch by a father refused access, and in the third second he realized all hell was going to break loose and he was after fucking up rightly. And he can't properly explain why it was only little Dylan going out the door to the play area at that second – why wasn't there a swarm of kids going out the door together the way there always is at playtime? Why was Dylan so far ahead? I don't *know*, I don't *know*, it all happened so *fast*, Philly says he keeps saying, and putting his fat fingers over his face and snotting and crying like a child.

THAT BOY OF the Hanrahans isn't half as thick as people make out. And better again, people don't edit themselves around him, thinking him to be an out and out God-help-us. That's how he picked up on that boy's words. The likes of Timmy do be invisible. I'll have to start putting these feelings into words properly soon. Philly will have a right laugh at me. Good man Jim, he'll say, come on so and we'll jump at the word of a halfwit and a feeling in your gut. He'll tell me get back into my box the very same way he told me the time years ago when the rapid response lads were called out to that lad of the Cunliffes and he above in the farmhouse waving his shotgun at the neighbours. I'd have handled that the finest. He'd have done a few months wrapped up in a nice warm blanket above in Dundrum.

Them armed response lads blew that poor boy to Kingdom Come the very minute he set foot outside his front door. I'd have gotten that gun off of him no bother. That was nearly ten years ago and there was hardly a peep around here since. Madness must come around in ten-year cycles. That time, there was two shootings and a fatal car crash in the space of two months. Now we have another murder and a snatched child; well, a child *from* here snatched, and you can sense the potential for more. It's in the air, in the way people are moving around each other with grim faces and shining eyes, either all frantic activity or standing in tight groups, talking quietly and looking at the ground. This must be how things were the time of the war against the British, when a crowd outside of Mass would suddenly explode into a flying column, guns appearing from under overcoats, killers appearing from inside of ordinary people. They were good killings, though – the Tans burned churches and creameries, interfered with women and shot little children. That was a time when killing was for good, for God and country. That time is long gone. But aren't we still the same people?

Frank

THE FUTURE IS a cold mistress. You can give all your life looking to her and trying to catch a hold of her but she'll always dance away from your fingertips and laugh back at you from the distance. Them that says they know her are liars and thieves. What was ever wrote down on paper that came true, that could be checked? Not one thing since the Scriptures. That's what I was thinking about, sitting over there beside the stove on my old green chair when I heard the door going and that fucking hairy ape burst in here and walloped me with a plank of wood, proving my point in fine style. I hadn't time to know I was dying before I was dead. I went quare easy in the end, all the same. I thought I was in for a messy, drawn-out affair; I had visions of the county home and the Regional Hospital and oxygen masks and tubes sticking out of me and Paki doctors poking me with their bony, brown fingers. And Bobby sitting looking at me and not knowing whether to read me the newspaper or put a pillow over my face and smother me. I should be thankful for that big lad that lamped me, I suppose. I fairly lit his soul on fire that day. I stung him like a dying wasp. I always had a knack for hitting people where it hurt. Sometimes it was as if the words were whispered into my ear by the devil himself.

There was plenty around here thought they knew the future, thought they had her number, took her fully for granted. I even knew, long before that gorilla arrived in and did for me, that no man could be assured of what the next day would hold. There's no man on this earth can even be assured he'll *have* a next day. I often thought to tell Bobby that, especially a few years ago when he was going around cock of the walk about the place, acting like he was God's gift to the world on account of his being Pokey Burke's number one lapdog. What a thing to be proud of. I watched him when he arrived in that day and found me dead and dirty in a puddle of blood and shit. You lose control of yourself at the moment of your death; that's something I didn't know. He stood looking down at me and I stood beside him looking down at myself and I said: Good man Bobby. You're a good man, Bobby. You sees things more clearly too, through dead eyes. He flinched. I'd nearly swear he felt my dead breath on his face; he might have even heard my silent words. He picked up the plank of wood that the big lad had flung away from him. It was lying in the blood near my head. Then he rang that thick fucker Jim Gildea to come down and ballsed himself right up. That boy got his mother's brains. He hasn't a dust of sense.

I'M NEARLY SURE I've been dead about a month. I haven't got out past the front door yet. It'll be a fair old while before I'm left leave this limbo, I'd say. They probably don't know what to do with me. I'm stuck here while they wonder about it, them that does the deciding about who gets sent where. They'd want to get the finger out now, in all fairness. I'd say I'm meant to be contemplating my life and feeling sorry for my wrongdoing. The Vatican done away with Purgatory, I'd say that's why I'm being left here to haunt my own house. Ha! There's too much going on around here to allow for much contemplation. That blondie lady of the Cassidys with the fine big chest waltzed in to poke at me. I often seen her on the telly, going in to shitholes to look at dead wasters with her pink lipstick. She's a fine cut of a woman, so she is. I wish they could have tightened me up a bit before they left her in here. Then they carried me out in a pine coffin and I was nearly lonesome after myself. Bobby was back down after a few days looking like a kicked pup. They left him out on bail. The thick bollocks never told them he didn't do me in, obviously. Christ, if you saw him, the cut of him, when Jim Gildea arrived in here belly-first, looking at me out of his mouth and the plank of timber in his hand and my blood dripping off of it onto the floor. Jim Gildea asked him straight out was he after killing me and he told him he didn't know. I don't *know*, he said. Imagine that! What a stupid prick.

I WONDER am I meant to be having revelations. Or epiphanies. Or both. I wonder is this meant to be a punishment, to be confined to this cottage where I lived my whole life and where my father lived before me. I was full sure he'd still be knocking around here, you know, watching to make sure I wasn't getting notions. Maybe he was sent below. Ha! I wouldn't be surprised if he was, he'd have gave the devil himself a good run for his money on his best days. Most men would have built a big two-storey or a nice dormer bungalow on the land and made the old place into a slatted house. Wasters. Why would a man leave a house with walls as thick as a fortress to be a toilet for cattle and go and live in a cardboard box? To impress women, that's the only reason men ever did that. Imagine giving them cowboy builders thousands and thousands of pounds to scratch their arseholes for six months and make you a house out of bits of wood and blocks made of foreign stones! Bobby was talking out through his hole one time about building an extension onto the back. I told him the only extension that was needed around here was to the end of his mickey. Himself and that girl that married him were trying to have a child that time and his seed wasn't taking. The devil's whispers again.

I was never able to talk to that boy without upsetting him. His mother had a fool made out of him, kissing him and telling him he was beautiful every two minutes. I was forced to bring balance. I had to prepare him for the hard world. Where light shines a shadow is cast; that's an elementary thing that every boy must be taught, especially boys that are mollycoddled by their mothers. He'd have gotten some hop if I'd left him off out thinking he was the boy his mother told him he was. She only ever had eyes for him from his first day on this earth. She forgot about me the very minute she squeezed him out of herself. He fell out with her for a finish, though. That shook her! She had an awful complex about herself, anyway. A *superiority* complex. She was full sure she was a few cuts above me, that lady. She looked down through her nose at me every day we were wed until the very day she died. I often asked her to know how was it she married me in the first place. She never answered me, only went off sulking in one of the back rooms for herself, or stood in front of me with her eyes like two pools of wet, blue sadness. I couldn't ever stop at her.

The sadder she looked the faster the brutal sharp words flowed from me; some making tiny little nicks, more tearing deep into her. Her soul suffered death by a thousand million cuts. I knew I was doing it and I couldn't stop. God help us, I could never stop at either of them.

Still and all though, when my grandchild's eyes first met mine, a powerful weakness overtook me. I caught myself looking into the wispy-looking little basket they had him in and saying words of thanks inside in my head for him. I was afraid to open my mouth for fear my voice would betray me. I knew I hadn't it in me not to sound false or foolish or a kind of hollow, somehow. I turned my face away and left. I hardly saw that child again. Bobby called him after himself, you know. It wasn't off of me he got that vanity.

I LEARNT my lessons faster than Bobby. My father was a better teacher than me. I ran into the milking parlour straight from school one time when I was only a small boy. I had news bursting out of me that I thought would make him praise me. We were given a test in school today Daddy, I told him. Were ye now? He never turned around to look at me, only kept on pumping away at the old Dairymaster that he always said was only a balls of a yoke that he was tricked into buying by a Godless fuckin Proddie. Ya, the master gave us forty questions on history and geography and maths and all that. Did he now? Ya, and I was the only one got every single one of them right so I was. The *cigire* was there today, you see, and Sir didn't know he was coming at all and he was told give us the test and he was pure solid delighted with me for getting all the questions right on account of the *cigire* being there out of the blue. My father still didn't face me, but he went kind of still and his back straightened and he turned his face a little bit around so I could see his red cheek and his glistening eye. So you know it all, do you? A lead ball dropped into my stomach. I didn't know what answer to give to *that* question. Before I could open my stupid little mouth again my father had a length of Wavin pipe in his hand that he used to use to shcoo-up the cattle along the yard and it was going swish, *whack*, swish, *whack*, swish, *whack* against my little scrawny body and I couldn't see out through my eyes for the shock and the sudden pain of it; I fell out backwards through the parlour door onto the hard, mucky ground and my father was roaring: You. Know. NOTTEN. You. Know. NOTTEN. You. Know. NOTTEN. By the time my mother crept out to the yard and said stop it Francie in her mousy little voice there was no part of me not covered in pinky-white welts. My father stood back and spat on the ground and admired his handiwork. Bejaysus, you know something now, though. You know something now, boy. You know that pride is a deadly sin. And he threw the Wavin pipe on the ground and walked over me back into the parlour, the very same way as your man threw down his plank of wood and walked off after he pole-axed me.

THEY SAY violence begets violence, but that's not always true. I had no stomach for violence my whole life. I had to bluff my way out of a few tight spots. I often thought to take a stick to Bobby when he was losing the run of himself, but I wasn't able to tighten my fingers around any weapon I ever put my hand on to beat him with. That's an awful affliction for a man to have. Not even drink could lift that paralysis from me. I only ever done violence to *things*. I could only ever wound a person with my words. I practised for years and years until it was as natural to me as breathing. When I used to drink I used to have imaginings of killing men with my bare hands, fantasies of strength I knew I didn't have. I used to swallow whiskey like a dry, weary man slugging flat lemonade in a summer hayfield and I'd picture myself with my two hands around my father's throat, watching his face turning purple while his soul was squeezed out of him through his ear holes. Then I'd go pure solid mad and wreck all before me: chairs, tables, doors, windows. I'd leave holes in plaster running with my own blood. Imagine the waste of it, thinking about killing a dead man. I wonder will I see him again. I wonder does he know already there's only two acres left of his stinking, precious land, wild with briars and brambles, or will I have the pleasure of telling him how a share of the worth of his life's labour was gave in over the counter to every fat publican in five parishes. I wonder how is it I was able to do to Bobby exactly what was done to me, even with my useless hands bound by cowardice. I wonder how will I ever be reconciled to myself. I wonder how will I look upon the face of God.

Triona

MY AUNTIE BERNADETTE liked things to be unadorned and liturgically correct. Like the rough cross she had my cousin Coley carve from a limestone block. Coley wanted to smooth it and add Celtic rings and swirls to its front. He spent a whole day with his bony arse in the air as he chipped and hacked and sanded, an acute angle of unnatural adolescent concentration. Bernadette put a halt to his artisan's gallop with a savage flourish: she smacked him into the side of his head, sending his chisel flying from his hand and his sinful pride flying from his heart. It's fine as it is, she said. Leave it over at the top of the path by the front door, let you, so that all who enter here know we are followers of Christ. Fucking old c-cunt, spat Coley when she'd returned to baking her unleavened bread. I suddenly saw the beauty in him, as the darkness of anger and frustration threw his angular jaw and blazing eyes into sharper relief. I've always needed to be shocked into awareness.

Bobby was the first person ever to remind me of Coley. Like Coley, he'd never have said the things the other lads around here would say. He stood with but was never a part of the herd of donkeys. Hee-haw, hee-haw, look at the knockers on your wan! Hee-haw, hee-haw, Jaysus lads I'm *red* from riding! Hee-haw, hee-haw, fuck it lads, I'd *bate* it into her! Bobby was silent, tall, red-faced in summer and ghost-white in winter. I always knew him, years and years before he first spoke to me, standing on the sticky floor in front of the bar of the Cave inside in town. His nervousness shocked me; I'd always thought he'd thought he was too cool to talk to us. Then I was suddenly aware of all the other things behind his eyes: fear, doubt, shyness, sadness. I was wrapped in him from that minute. I'd never look at another man again. Mobiles were still fairly new in those days. Pokey Burke must have been one of the first to get dumped by text.

Bernadette would fry pieces of chicken in their own juice and serve them with boiled green beans and unleavened bread. When my parents dropped me over there to be minded I ate the Communion of the Faithful at every meal. Bernadette never went to Mass; she was a *fundamentalist* Christian. Mother often said she only used religion as a framework for her craziness. She could just as easily have been a Muslim or a Buddhist or a white witch. She hung around with some group of Bible-bashers inside in town. They met in a leaking, groaning flat and read all the best bits from Genesis to Revelations, slowing down to a near stop at Leviticus. Bernadette used The Word to torture Coley, just as Frank used his own spiteful words to torment Bobby. Coley didn't survive Bernadette's terrible reign over his childhood. At a tender, gangly fourteen he hung himself from the branch of an elder in their back garden that looked hardly stout enough to hold his weight. Bobby only barely survived Frank. Every time I met Frank I got the ghostly smell of unleavened bread baking; I could almost taste its thin dryness in my mouth. There was a spinning heart on the gate at the front of their house, a mocking symbol, Bobby's rough cross.

I WOULDN'T CARE if Bobby never again brought a cent into this house. Earlier in the summer, when the whole village had it that he was going with that girl from Pokey's ghost estate, I couldn't have cared less; I knew he wouldn't betray me in a million years. When he wouldn't talk to me after they left him out on bail, though, I could have killed him. I screamed at him, into his face, over and over again to just *talk*, please, please just *talk* to me. I don't even care if he *did* kill Frank. I wouldn't love him any less. I'd perjure myself for him without breaking a sweat. I'd swear on a Bible and lie through my teeth in a heartbeat. Why wouldn't I? I'd use the same Good Book that Bernadette used to bruise poor Coley's soul.

Bobby hated his father and never got over his mother and thought of himself as a failure for not protecting her properly from his father's cruel tongue. His putdowns put her in the ground. It took me three years to get that much from him. I asked Bobby early on why he'd fallen out with his mother. He said they stopped talking, not to be drawing his father on them, and they just got stuck in that auld way. *Stuck in that auld way?* Well that makes no sense, I said. He just said I know it doesn't, I know it doesn't. Bobby whispers when what he's saying upsets him. Then he stops. I learned quickly. I never pressed him to say anything until after the Frank thing. All of our years together, I never pushed, I just let him feel that I knew his pain was there and that I'd help him with it and there was no rush, no need to tell me anything until he wanted to. He had the words; I knew that. Bobby always read a lot.

Every now and again, and with no trigger that I could ever figure out, Bobby would start to tell me things. A few times I was just asleep when he started talking, in that kind of dozing where you're not fully unconscious but still able to dream, maybe even with your book still in your hand. Bobby's soft voice, as gentle as it is, would be shocking in its suddenness in the silent room, and I'd try not to move so as not to put him off. Even a start of alarm, or sitting up too quickly, or putting my hand out to him, or trying to encourage him would snap him out of whatever spoken daydream had overtaken him to allow him to speak to me about the things I wanted him to so badly. Thinking about it now, the dead stillness I'd assume, the way I'd almost hold my breath while he spoke, it was the very same as when I'd be trying not to startle a wild animal that had wandered into the garden. That's the only way I could help him with his pain, imagine. To lie there in silence, not moving a muscle.

It's not like he even said anything that would sound to someone from outside as being all that terrible. I mean to say, Frank never laid a finger on him or his mother. It was just the life of awful, awful coldness, and the constant wearing down of their spirits, a gloomy, nervy slog of a life, punctuated by days and nights of mad rage when he'd wreck the house and Bobby's mother would grab him and run for it, just in case he forgot himself altogether and took at *them* as well as the furniture and the crockery. But it was always all too far down in Bobby for it not to cut and wound on the way out. I sometimes believe on those nights that he spoke about things that he was forcing himself to do it just for my benefit, that he was suffering the reliving of that keen-edged sadness and regret because he thought I wanted him to say it out, because of some notions he thought I had of the healing and redemptive power of talking things out. But all I could really do was lie there and listen and think: this is Bobby, this is my husband.

I have one memory of Frank that will always abide, though, when all the other memories are faded to a series of blurred impressions, the way memories of a book will fade, even one that gripped you so much that you couldn't sleep until you finished it. It was the club awards ceremony the year the lads were robbed of the county championship. One of the old boys from Ciss Brien's front bar had written a song of never-ending verses called 'The Ballad of Bobby Mahon'. It was just a silly thing, really, a bit of craic to raise people's spirits, the kind of thing that's been done a thousand times for a thousand village heroes. He set the words to the tune of 'The Wearing of the Green'. After Bobby had been given his shield for being the club's player of the year and had mumbled his pride and apologies, *apologies* imagine, into the microphone on the little stage against the back wall of the Munster, the words he'd learned by rote drowned out by the cheers of the parish, the old boy and a few session players struck up the song. I could see that Bobby was mortified. He didn't know where to look. But I knew by his smile and his eyes that he was happy, too, as if it was only in that moment that he'd realized how much people thought of him and how no one blamed him for losing the final, and how all these rowdy, clapping, laughing people knew he'd drawn and shed and sweated blood for them, more than anyone. And then he looked along the length of that packed room, over the heads of the half-drunk, bellowing crowd, and his face changed. In a way that only I could see. And when I turned and followed his gaze, I saw Frank, and he was just inside the door, wearing an expression of contempt; a twisted half-smile that plainly said: You fool. This is a room full of fools, and you're chief among them. And I hated him in those seconds more than any other time. More even than when he'd looked into baby Robert's crib and said not a word. I felt like jumping up from my seat and throwing myself on him and wringing his mangy old neck, scratching the blackness from his eyes. But afterwards, after thinking and thinking about it, I wondered: why was he there at all? What brought him in to stand just inside the door of the Munster Tavern and watch his son? And even though I was so raging with him for casting a shadow on Bobby's moment, I started for the first time to think that there was more inside in Frank than just spite.

I tried to never do it, but I constantly compared Frank to my own father and felt an awful, hollow bitterness at Frank's continued existence, festering in the dark inside of that cottage, tormenting Bobby daily still, after all the years lived and all the words said and not said. Some people, like Bobby, take on the troubles of others and others can't see anything past their own. Isn't there something to be said all the same for everyone just minding their own business? When my father got really sick all he worried about was me and my mother and whether I was able to keep up my work and study and whether I was worrying about him and no one was to worry about him and there was no fear of him and did Joe Brien drop up that load of blocks and make sure your mother knows to pay Joe from the money in the locked drawer on the left-hand side of the desk and the key is at the back corner of the drawer on the right-hand side and tell her not to use money from her purse and was she checking the slips every month to know was the ESB paying out his proper pension and was the health insurance still being paid automatically. He was a constant worrier, and never about himself. Thank God it was Bobby I fell for, and not someone who would have added to his worries. He was stone mad about Bobby. They could sit in a room together and watch a match and not even talk, except for a few bits of shouts and cheers and tuts and sighs here and there. They never felt the need to make idle conversation, to talk for talk's sake. Bobby loved just sitting in the same room as him. I think they were an ease to each other.

My father told me once, not long before he died, that he couldn't keep the passing days straight in his mind. That was the first time I was really frightened for him, that I got a sense of what was coming. Bobby and I weren't married long. He'd been to see a new GP in the village and she'd told him to do all the things he enjoyed doing, to not think about what food was good for his health and what wasn't, to have a drink if he felt like it. She was being kind, and she smiled at him and touched his hand gently, but her words frightened the life out of him, more than any of the talk from the doctors inside in the Regional Hospital about the size of tumours and their rapid growth and the pressure they exerted on organs and their explanations of how the machine worked that he lay down inside in, with his eyes closed tight and his fists clenched as if to fight against the fear he had of being in that hollow tube, nearly naked and fully alone, closed in on all sides.

My goose is cooked, he said, on the way home from the village, as he looked out the passenger side window at the Arra Mountains in whose vale he'd lived his whole life. Ah boys. And he laughed gently. And that was as much as he ever said of his fear or his sadness. I was afraid to open my mouth to speak. I should have said no Dad, there's loads of fight left in you yet, you have years and years, come on, please, don't just give up. But those words would have been for me and not him. For all my talk, I had nothing to say.

Frank shook my hand at Daddy's funeral and looked straight into my eyes and said he was very sorry for my trouble. And he kind of smiled at me. I couldn't even say thanks to him. God forgive me, all I could think was: why couldn't you have died instead, Frank?

BOBBY WAS never able to see how he affected people. People always saw what they wanted to see in Bobby. He could never see the way people reacted to him. The adoration of the young lads, the respect of the builders, the misty-eyed devotion of the old codgers who roared themselves raw from the sidelines while he led a team of committed losers to the gates of glory. But still and all, songs and pints and backslapping nights of praise and speeches aside, some people will hate you for your goodness. They'll revel in your undoing. They'll rejoice at the news of your downfall. It felt to me as though that was the way everyone was this summer. I couldn't see the good in anyone. I stood one day in the post office queue and Robert was wriggling and whining and I hadn't showered and my roots were in shit and the story about Bobby having the affair was flapping around like a crow with a broken wing and I saw one of the Teapot Taliban staring at me with *rapture* on her face.

People say things like we shouldn't complain lads, look at that poor girl whose child was stole. People say things like shouldn't we be counting our blessing lads that we at least have our health? People say things like look at that poor girl of the Mahons, Bobby's wife, and he after doing the dirty on her and killing his father and she still with him. Bobby Mahon done the dirt. He killed his father. The girl he done the dirt with is after having her child snatched. How many of them really cared about the little boy? He was only young Seanie Shanahan's bastard. That lady is only a blow-in from town, a right-looking little rap. Everyone talked about him and looked all sad and serious in Mass when he was prayed for and joined in the search and made sandwiches and shook their heads mournfully and asked how in God's name that girl was coping, but deep, deep down some of them were more worried about their pensions and medical cards and wages and profits and welfare payments and what they haven't that their neighbours have and who's claiming what and how many foreigners were allowed in to the country and the bottom line is the bottom line as far as I can see; if we were all in the black we'd all be in the pink. The air is thick with platitudes around here. We'll all pull together. We're a tight-knit community. We'll all support each other. Oh really? Will we?

The Teapot Taliban fattened on their stories about Bobby and that girl. And she had the child for young Sean Shanahan, imagine! What a triangle! Or is it a square? Ha ha ha! When Frank was killed they must have nearly exploded with pleasure. Now! He *is* only an animal! Who'd have thought he'd stoop that low? Blood will out, the father was a desperate quare hawk too, God rest him! Jesus, the sweet scandal, it must have been almost too rich for their pill-thinned blood. It could have easily caused embolisms. Their eyes glistened with glee in the post office queue. They looked at me and tut-tutted and whispered and nodded and shook their heads and counted off blessings on their rosary beads. They wondered was Bobby the snatched child's father. They wondered was it Bobby snatched the child. They wondered how was it they never knew he was a madman. Poor Triona, they said, and she stuck in the middle of all that. Poor Triona, they said, but secretly they were delighted for me, with my fine dormer bungalow on the lovely site Bobby got for a song off of the Burkes, swanning around the place in my big oh-eight car. My cough was after getting well and truly softened. The missing child didn't put anything into perspective for anyone the way they were all saying it did, he was just tacked on to the end of the list of things that just showed you how terrible it all is and how the country is pure solid destroyed and there's no end to the heartbreak and aren't we a right show now with the television cameras and the place crawling with guards. God, I'm gone awful cross. People are scared, that's all. I know that.

THE CHILD'S little body was covered in weird marks when he was found a few days ago: pentagrams and crosses and lines from poems and drawings of naked people, all in permanent marker, like tattoos drawn by a lunatic. He was wearing Spiderman pyjamas. His hair was all shaved off; he looked like a little refugee from a concentration camp. Mary Gildea had the whole story. The whole village had it inside an hour. It was her husband Jim who found the child. He spotted something in one of the guys who helped with the search. He couldn't put his finger on it; he just had a feeling. And Timmy Hanrahan brought him some piece of evidence that confirmed his hunch. Our Timmy, imagine! Jim followed the guy until he led him to a flat inside in town. Jim called no one else in to help, only walked straight in the door behind that guy and there was little Dylan, sitting on a beanbag watching a DVD of *Bob the Builder*, and the fat Montessori teacher sitting beside him, feeding him a bowl of ice-cream. Jim picked him up in his arms and walked back out the door and the two freaks didn't even try to stop him. He was fine except for the drawings all over him and the skinned head. They'll wash off and his hair will grow back and he'll forget all about the whole thing. May he always be fine and happy, the little darling.

WHEN I TOLD Bobby the child had been found safe and sound he said nothing. He stood looking out the back window at our little Robert, screaming for joy as he tried to catch a fat pigeon that was fluttering madly in the birdbath. Tears spilled down his face. I just said oh love; oh love, what matters now?

What matters only love?

Acknowledgments

THANKS: To Antony Farrell and everyone at the Lilliput Press, especially Sarah Davis-Goff and Daniel Caffrey; to Brian Langan, Eoin McHugh and all at Doubleday Ireland; to Marianne Gunn O'Connor; to my earliest readers: Frances Kelly, Dermot Dinan, Brian Treacy, Paul Fenton, Shauna Nugent, Conor McAllister, Brendan Ryan, Carmel O'Reilly, Helena Enright, Bríd Enright, Marie Cremin and Kathryn McDermott; to Conor Cremin and Garry Browne for their friendship and unflagging encouragement; to my parents, Anne and Donie Ryan, for everything; to my sister Mary, my first reader and most ardent promoter; to my brother John and nephew Christopher, of whom I'm endlessly proud; to my beautiful children, Thomas and Lucy, for giving me the heart to persevere; and to Anne Marie, the love of my life.